Alpha's Daughter Rejected

Vickie H. Tokin

The Exiled Alpha

VICKIE H. TOKIN

ALPHA'S DAUGHTER
REJECTED

Table of Contents

Alpha's Daughter Rejected

Introduction

Cassie Mora: 17 werewolf. Silver eyes and dark blonde hair that reaches her butt make her threatening. Alpha markings on her back extend up to her neck. speaks French, Spanish, and Romanian. most relaxed in the outdoors, especially on or near water. Trust problems. street fighter on the side. Pack: Oregon's rising moon. Lucy the wolf

Ari Mora: 36 Werewolf. Cassie's mother. Short, dark blonde hairstyle. eyes that are blue. rational; composed. not marked. most at ease in a wooded area. Pack: Oregon's rising moon. Jessie the wolf

Axe Drageste: 18. Werewolf. blonde hair cut short. One eye is oceanic blue and the other is emerald green. Sarcastic. enjoys archery. over the breast and back, an alpha symbol. asleep in bed, the happiest. Pack: North Carolina's secret moon. Alex the Wolf

Cole Peck: 37 Werewolf. black hair cut short. grey eyes. Stubborn. Back has Alpha marks. Black moon of Tennessee pack. Nick, the wolf's name.

Alpha's Daughter Rejected: Chapter 1

Cassie's POV

The day was ordinary. I give my mother a kiss on the cheek when I get home from training, leaving my boots at the door. But that wasn't an ordinary day. Mom had a phone call. Now, what makes that odd? You query. The strange thing wasn't that mum was on the phone. It was strange since she was about to start crying. Mom never sheds a tear.

I sat down in the nearby recliner after setting my bag down next to it. Mom closes the phone, and I must have had a puzzled expression on my face because she immediately begins speaking.

"That was grandfather for you. He called to let me know that he and his mother had finally divorced. Babe, he requests that we pay him a visit. She finally says after a brief pause.

"Mom. You able to manage that? Will He be present? I inquire in regard to the pack's leader. He was, at least, until my mother departed with me. He was intended to be her mate, but he turned her down while she was one month pregnant. I don't want my mother around him because he injured her.

"I can manage it, yes. Furthermore, getting to know your grandfather and uncle will be beneficial for you. He was still the alpha when I last checked, so I assume he will be present. She chuckled as she stated.

Why has your father suddenly decided to enter our lives? I inquire in total confusion. For 17 years, he couldn't bear the concept of being near us, and now all of a sudden he wants to be there. Why?"

"You know what, we can talk about it later. He wasn't the one who-" Please phone in and pack up so they know you won't be at training.

, "Yes, ma'am." I say stomping off infuriated. "Hey. I cherish you.

"I love you, too, baby girl."

I up the stairs and begin packing—mostly tank tops—while also placing calls. I quickly finish packing and cancel my training for the upcoming two weeks.

What time do we depart?

"At noon tomorrow. He wants to speak with me right away. Mom advised against staring at me.

"Is he aware that I exist?" I ask my mother, attempting to get her attention.

"Well, no, but I kept it a secret. My mother abandoned me, and he rejected me. I simply never had the chance to share anything about it with anyone. Still not looking into my eyes, she continued.

I comprehend. I'm going for a run, hello. I promise to return before midnight. As I put my shoes on, I say. I've always found that running relieves my tension, and I could use that right now. I understand why my mother kept my existence a secret, but the prospect of Him making an appearance makes my skin crawl. I've read and heard a lot about Him. that he was a player and that he was nasty when he was angry. The idea of that man around my mother makes me sick to my stomach.

I can hear the neighboring creek as I rush through the pack territory's forest. I approach it and take my shoes off. Sitting in the woods with my feet in a stream is the most soothing thing I can imagine. I do just that, then. I recline, close my eyes, and inhale deeply. I can see eyes peering back at me as soon as I close my eyes. I'm sure that these are my friends.

One partner exists for werewolves. You can be paired again if your partner rejects you, like my mother's did. Luna, the goddess of the moon, is a thoughtful creature. She is aware of heartache. If, like my mother, you decide not to locate a new partner, you will be bound to that person forever. However, you spend a month just staring into your partner's eyes before you finally meet. I should see him soon because I've been seeing them for a few weeks now.

When I opened my eyes again, the day had drastically changed, so I know I dozed off. I'm grateful that I wear shorts and tank tops to training at times like these. The lines shouldn't be too noticeable if I tan because I hadn't yet changed.

I get up, put on my shoes and socks, and walk back to my house. Even though it's only 10:25, I'm already hungry because the alpha is coming over for supper. Even though I'm likely running late, I'm not as stressed as usual for dinner with the alpha. There is never really a cause; things just happen.

The Alphas truck is already there when I arrive, but since it's still warm, they haven't been here for very long. They are talking to their mother on the couch when I go in. I give them a nod before heading upstairs to get ready. It takes me about 5 minutes to complete the aforementioned, and then I head back down the stairs after changing into a tank top and some shorts. We all hastily say hello to me before sitting down at the table.

"So, Alpha Liam, my father has gotten in touch with me and wants my permission to go see the Black moon pack. He would appreciate the opportunity to get to know me after all these years of being apart because my mother and father were divorced. Of course, I'd bring Cassie along so she could meet her uncle and grandfather. With the greatest respect, my mum says.

Liam turns to face his wife, Lilly, whose eyes had engulfed her head, after first looking at my mother. Before speaking, she turns her head from my mother to me and back again.

Are you certain, Ari, my love, that you won't experience excruciating pain while traveling there? You are aware of the possibilities, right? Lilly adds as she gives my mum a concerned look. Lilly had been a better mother than my own grandmother, despite the fact that they were almost the same age. She never contested my claim that she was my aunt. She supported it in fact.

"I can promise you that I am prepared and fully aware of what might occur. With Cas by my side, I'm confident I can handle it. mother said.

Does He know she's there? Alpha Liam inquires while warily glancing at my mother.

"No, he doesn't. In less than a year, when she turns 18, she may choose whether or not she wants him in her life. I won't hinder her. My mum continued speaking in a professional tone.

"I don't." Since I know they heard me, I speak rapidly.

"Therefore, I have no issues with you going to see your father and brother. with one caveat. Says Alpha Liam.

"Yes?" Mom and I agree on this.

Less than 30 minutes separate the Black moon pack house from the Hidden moon pack house. I much prefer that you remain there. I am aware that the previous alpha has been replaced by his son. They would happily make room for you. He says while holding Aunt Lilly's hand and addressing my mother and I.

Naturally, Alpha. Mom tells me.

"Therefore, you have my approval. When do you intend to depart? He calmly poses a few more questions.

"At noon tomorrow." Mom claims.

We'll be there to say good-bye. Be safe, please, my beloved. says Alpha Lilly.

"I am always." Mom says as she embraces her.

While the adults chat over coffee after dinner and I quickly finish my meal, I drift off to sleep daydreaming about a stunning pair of eyes.

Alpha's Daughter Rejected: Chapter 2

Cassie's POV

Well, the morning went by without incident. We bid the Alphas Liam and Lilly farewell before boarding the pack's private jet. The toughest thing in the world was getting my phone turned off. I didn't do it because I was addicted, but rather because I was waiting for The Coordinator to call. At least, that's what we called him. He coordinated all of the werewolf street fights. Joe is the name I gave him. After all, he did go by that name.

I'm looking forward to getting off the plane and stretching my legs after the roughly 10-hour flight, which includes a few layovers. To be honest, however, it's still uncomfortable to sit for so long, even on a private plane. And let's not even talk about the cuisine. That crap tastes worse than the food from school.

When we DO FINALLY touch down, I theatrically rush out of the plane and begin flipping and doing cartwheels while my mother rolls her eyes. She is accustomed to my pranks and enjoys my spasticity. This one is dripping with sarcasm.

When we enter the airport, we are greeted by two smiling people holding a sign with our last name on it. We saunter (because who walks?) over to them, and when I glance at my mother, she has a slight smile on her face.

I take it that you two represent Alpha and Beta. Mom comments as she surveys the males in front of us.

"The Gamma and the Beta, ma'am. The alpha needed to take care of business. The blonde said with a smile. "This is Riley, the gamma, and I'm James, the beta."

James, it's nice to meet you. This is Cassie, my kid, and I'm Ari. Mom says as she extends her hand, and I do the same.

I shake hands and say, "Cas for short."

Okay, now, if you'll just follow us, there's a car waiting for us outside. stated Riley. He's not ugly, really. Both of them are not. Riley is exactly 6' tall and has red hair and green eyes, whereas James is around 6'2" and blonde with brown eyes. There is no doubt that neither of them is older than 25.

I'm curious in the type of business the alpha had to handle. Mom queries me via a mind link.

Most likely obtaining authorization to enter Grandpa's pack. I answer.

Maybe, but the first time we enter, just the two of us. We're entering alone at first, but I don't mind if others join us later. Before we flood your grandfather with people from another pack, I want you to meet him. She clarifies.

As we get in the car, I say, "Yeah, no, I get it."

So, how does the Risen moon pack feel like? We haven't visited in some time. Jim enquires.

"I truly like it. The fight squad has really improved recently, and the surroundings are amazing. Mom mentions the combat squad while glancing at me. She takes great satisfaction in me because I train the beginners as well as the top athletes.

"Really? According to what I've heard, the combat squad recently hired a new trainer. Have you already met them? Riley queries as she looks back at her mother in the rearview mirror.

"Really, yes. You have, too, but you're not yet aware of it. Making eye contact with him, according to Mom.

"Really?" Jim queries.

"It's me." I say. I don't like to be coy or act innocent. 'I'm not Willy Wonka,' I like to say. I don't mince words.

"Seriously? Then you'll need to demonstrate some of your moves for us. Riley explains. "It's been a difficult year. We lost our teacher and his partner last year, and we haven't been able to locate somebody to fill their position. He only had daughters, and he was getting older, which was sad. They both got partners, and they don't want to see them argue.

Who has been instructing the training, then? I query bewildered. You haven't been dormant for a year, right?

Of course not, but none of the older students who were instructing the younger students could compare to him. James clarifies.

Before we get to the pack house, we talk about some other crap for around 30 minutes. The aroma of fried chicken greets us right away.

We made you a dinner since we thought you might be hungry, so the pack cook made it. What's typically served for dinner in the South? My mother interrupted James before he could finish.

"I don't mean to be impolite, but I grew up 30 minutes away from here, and I realize it doesn't really matter. Cassie was raised on southern cuisine because I couldn't bear to live without it. We are aware of what a southern dinner entails.

"Sure, that. I apologize, it seems I forgot. Blushing, he said.

"Mom, that was impolite."Sorry, baby doll, but I'm hungry and exhausted. It was still rude. I simply want to eat, not hear about the meal I'm going to consume. Please apologize. "I'm sorry. I was really nasty to say that. I'm just exhausted, and when I'm exhausted, I get cranky. We appreciate your kindness in preparing a supper for us. Mom genuinely stated.

"It really is nothing," James remarked while once again blushing.

When we arrive at the mansion, we are given a tour and escorted to our rooms before being instructed to relax in because supper is still being prepared. Since I smell too much like other people, I decide to take a shower. I quickly put on a straightforward grey v-neck t-shirt and some black skinny pants after taking a brief shower. I went downstairs after putting on my mid-calf boots to find my mother there already conversing with an elderly woman.

"There she is, I see. This is Cassie, my daughter. Mom tells the elderly women. Although I refer to her as older, she can't possibly be older than 40, if that. You can call me Cas, although my name is Cassandra. I am the mother of the current Alpha.

It's a pleasure to meet you. I'm Cassie, although most people call me Cas, so I'm sorry if I reply when they mean to speak to you. I say expressing regret up front.

Oh, and they might be speaking to my husband as well. There is constant confusion around here since even though his name is Caspian, most people just call him Cas. The speaker laughs.

"Well, this is going to be interesting." I'm laughing.

After dinner, we chat for a while before Cassandra announces that it is time for bed. Everyone pays attention to the head of the household. I sat down after going to my room and donning my pajamas, a black cami, and some teal and black shorts. After pacing about restlessly for approximately two hours, I decide to get up and get some water. Why not? It's only one in the morning.

Alpha's Daughter Rejected: Chapter 3

Cassie's POV

After dinner, we chat for a while before Cassandra announces that it is time for bed. Everyone pays attention to the head of the household. I sat down after going to my room and donning my pajamas, a black cami, and some teal and black shorts. After pacing about restlessly for approximately two hours, I decide to get up and get some water. Why not? It's only one in the morning.

I stealthily descend the stairs and make my way to the kitchen, where I obtain a glass and get a cup of water. I drink my water, clean it, and lay the glass upside-down on the drying rack before I hear a faint sound that I immediately recognize as footsteps. Unaware, they are the quiet-seeking actions of someone who is succeeding to some extent, but I'm better. In time to observe a figure round the corner into the living room, I stealthily turn around and move toward the edge of the kitchen. The distinct sound of a body falling onto a leather couch can be heard a brief while later.

According to the sound of skin on leather, I can hear the body shifting a little bit before it eventually settles down after a minute. Because they wouldn't have awakened everyone up, it is obvious that the body is not that of an invader. I detect a familiar smell, but I'm not sure what it is. Maybe it's raining on such a hot day? nevertheless, not quite. I decide to overlook it for the time being and look into it later as I head back up the stairs when a floorboard starts to squeak. If the sounds are any indication, this grabs the body's attention and causes it to sit up.

I turn back without trying to escape since I know I've been found. Running would cause the entire home to become awake, which is something I would like to prevent.

Asking "Who's there?" The question is whispered. I can now tell that he is clearly a male and that he is exhausted. I don't even try to respond; instead, I walk over to him.

I quickly know that this man is my match after he meets me halfway. I could do worse, to be completely honest. As I do the same to him, he looks over at me with his breath caught in his throat.

Oh yeah, there are worse things I could do. He is roughly 6'4" tall, with short blond hair, and has a lean build. Now for the real surprise. His eyes are heterochromatic. One of them is oceanic blue, while the other is emerald green. I could gaze into them for hours because they are so incredibly beautiful. His lips are full, and I have no doubt that his jaw could have been made of paper due to how sharp it was. Once more scanning his face, I note that he is still holding his breath and appears to be biting his tongue.

"You okay over there?" I ask as softly as I can to avoid waking up everyone in the home.

Just trying to avoid being cliche. He says while inhaling deeply.

So, may we speak? like maybe have a meal and get to know each other?" I inquire, and as he appears to be scared about being rejected, he visibly calms down.

Yes, that would be fantastic. The living room, perhaps? He makes a suggestion and sounds uneasy. We enter the living room and take a seat on the same couch, facing one another. We are both seated cross-legged on the opposite ends of the couch.

"Perhaps it's time for an introduction. My name is Cassie Mora. I'm 17 years old and am here with my mother from another pack. We're here to visit some long-lost relatives. I say plainly.

Axe Dragoste here. The pack's Alpha and I are both 18 years old. It is a privilege to meet you. Your alpha is very complimentary of you. He says taking my hand, which I had extended, and kissing it against his lips. Since we sat back down, he hasn't taken his eyes off of mine. I apologize for all the stares. I have a strong sense that this is a dream. I've only ever seen your eyes there, and I'm completely enthralled by them.

I understand how you feel. However, I do have to speak with you about something. I say.

"Ok." He says cautiously.

Get that idea out of your head, I'm not rejecting you. He takes a great breath of relief in response to what I say. "I'm warning you, though, that perhaps now isn't the greatest time to accept you. Currently, I'm quite busy, so when I do accept you, I want to be able to give you my undivided attention. I want to be able to put what I was taught as a child—that your partner is the most important thing—into practice. We are going to keep our relationship a secret for the time being, but I would never reject you and I would love to get to know you.

"Let me check that I understand this. For the time being, you can't accept me as your mate because of your confusing motivations for coming here, but you will once everything is worked out in public. He says, pauses, and waits for my affirmation before moving on. And you're not going to tell anybody because...?

"I don't want them to think I'm rejecting you, and right now, they don't need to know what my mother's doing here," he continued. As far as your pack is concerned, we are staying here at our alpha's request since we are visiting family. I say plainly. If my mother wants others to know more, she will explain.

Can you tell me how much deeper it is? He queries. As my mate, the alpha who is lending us his home, and for being so understanding of our situation, he has earned that right.

"I was the result of two friends having a one-night stand. The very next morning, my father rejected my mum. My father... is the pack leader, which is why we're staying here. We don't know how he'll respond because my mother recently received approval from the previous alpha to move even though she was already planning to move soon after the incident. When she learned, she was enrolled in our current pack's medical program. She had always been despised by her mother, who expelled her from the family after learning that she had been rejected. We are coming to visit her because her mother and father recently got divorced.

"Does anyone in her old pack even know you exist?" He asks with a startled expression on his face.

"Nope. Mom didn't even find out she was pregnant until she arrived in Oregon, and since she didn't really have any acquaintances here, she didn't phone anyone. I shrug and say.

We continue to chat while sitting about for a few more hours before we get too exhausted. We decide to get to know one another better by coming back here tomorrow. I stand up to go to my room, but before I do, I give him a short kiss on the cheek and then turn to walk upstairs. I sincerely hope that this wasn't a dream.

Alpha's Daughter Rejected: Chapter 4

Cassie's POV

Even though I only slept for approximately four hours last night, it was one of the nicest sleeps I've had in a very long time. No matter how little sleep I get the night before, I always seem to wake up at five in the morning, Oregon time. For my benefit, it implies it was 8 a.m. in North Carolina, which is a respectable time for them to wake up here. Actually, they had breakfast at that time.

Ladies, good morning! You slept well, I hope? said Cassandra.

"We definitely did. Once more, I appreciate your hospitality. My mother, who has always been a proponent of extreme politeness, remarks. I'm happy to state that I mostly inherited such quality.

"Wonderful! And there is no issue. Please join us in the dining room, if you don't mind. We are having a large family breakfast now that my husband, son, and father-in-law have returned from the business they had to finish.

That sounds fantastic. Could you please let me know who will be attending? My mother inquires, possibly attempting to determine whether we ought to get dressed.

The majority of my family, including my oldest son, the beta and gamma, and my siblings. My eldest son no longer resides in our home. He actually just got home from college. He lives in a house nearby.

"Wasn't it your son you said was the alpha?" I inquire, for the first time interjecting.

"Yes, Axe, my second-eldest son. My oldest kid claimed he didn't want it, so he took control. Power has never really appealed to him. With a little smile, she says. I'll admit that when I heard my friend's name, a shudder ran down my spine that I had to fight against. Will he allow us to meet him? A few things need to be discussed. She is told by my mother.

Yes, but before then, will you kindly join us for breakfast? She explains and shows us to the dining room from the previous evening. Three persons, two boys and a girl, are seated in a row in it.My three children are these three. Ryan, my oldest, Emily, my only female, and Easton, my youngest.

The head of the table and the seat to her right are left vacant while she takes a seat in the seat next to it on her right. The two chairs across from her, the head of the table on the other side, and the seat to its left are all vacant as well. The side opposite to Cassandra has her daughter on one side and her boys on the other. The only available seat at that end is beside Ryan because the Beta and Gamma are on the same side as Emily. I follow my mother to the seat next to her and take a position behind the table as she moves to the head of the table at that end. My training has taught me to wait to take a seat until my superiors have done so.

Not that it's difficult to hear footfall as they literally stomp into the room, but we soon hear them. The first stomper to show up is an older-looking man Cassandra stood up for, and when he gazed into her eyes, they began to glow with love. One can only infer that Caspian is her mate. Although he is fairly attractive and not the worst-looking beast, I must admit that Axe looks much better.

The fragrance of rain on the scorching pavement suggests that the devil is approaching. Strange odor, but all of my favorite moments have taken place just as it started to rain. He enters the room sporting some sweatpants and a white v-neck. I have to try not to gaze as it demonstrates his muscles. We just met, and the mate bond is killing me already. He nods to his family, smiles at my mother and me, and then moves to take a seat again. His seat is to the left of his moms and across from his fathers. The final member of their party enters as I was gently eyeing my mate. It turned to face him with respect and couldn't help but respond.

The phrase "Grandpa Whiskey?" I mutter in disbelief. He gives me a moment of his bewildered attention before his face lights up with recognition.

'D.P.!!" I can't help but run towards him as soon as he reacts and offers his arms for an embrace. I've only ever acted foolishly around him. My mum approaches us in a composed manner. How are you two doing? How long has it been since I last saw you guys?

It's been a little less than 10 years, and we're doing well. He replies as he encircles my mother with one arm, never releasing go of me in the process.

That would account for why I nearly missed recognizing my little gem right here. My, how you've developed. You resemble your mother in beauty virtually. He kisses my forehead and says. What brings you two here, then?

I asked, "Whiskey, why don't we let them eat first?" Cassandra approaches.

"Sure," you say. I naturally accepted his move for me to occupy the seat between him and Axe. The food is served while Mom makes her way back to her original seat at the opposite head of the table.

After a filling breakfast, my mother, all the officials, and I walked to the office and got to talking about everything. We talked about how this was going to work after she described how she had been rejected and left pregnant. We also had some disagreements over how my mother and I would travel alone the first day, with the boys being allowed to accompany us on the second and any consecutive days, but we eventually to an understanding. In other words, mom insisted that we go alone, we talked over it for five minutes, and then mom and Axe decided that the boys would drop us off at the meeting place and then go back, but that we would travel directly there and back. Everyone failed to ask us how we knew Grandpa Whiskey, so I predict that when we go back, that will be in doubt. The rest of the day was spent catching up and talking. As I got to know Axe better, I stayed up late talking to him. The day was enjoyable.

Alpha's Daughter Rejected: Chapter 5

Cassie's POV

I got up at five the following morning and went for a run. I had talked to Axe till so late that it wasn't a lengthy one, but I wanted to be energized to meet my long-lost family. The Beta and the Gamma will drive us to the border today so that mum can speak with the Alpha there. When we're through, we're to head straight to her father's house and then return. Mom, however, keeps mentioning a tiny ice cream business that she just adored and wants to check to see if it is still open.

Before I had a chance to fully process what is happening, we have already left and arrived at the meeting place. Before we arrive, the Beta and Gamma exit the vehicle and greet the driver before approaching. The Gamma then opens the door for my mother as the Beta resumes driving.

When she exits, he briefly exhibits complete shock, but he quickly covers it up. His entire stance has stiffened, and I can see that his wolf is struggling for dominance. After a brief exchange of words, he questions why they haven't departed after glancing at the automobile, whose windows are tinted.

Mom gives them one more moment to thoroughly trash each other while they wait for her to dismiss them before motioning for me to exit the vehicle. I exit the vehicle and close the door, doing my best to reveal my face. When I do eventually reveal my face to him, his mouth opens and his eyes nearly swallow his head.

"Who's this?" After a brief pause, when the shock has finally subsided, he inquires. It's evident that I'm related to him, but I believe he may be denying it or seeking confirmation; yet, that would be the simple solution and not at all dramatic. And my mother doesn't sound like that at all.

This warrior is the best in my group, I say. Knowing that wasn't what he was asking, my mum responds.

The question "Who are her parents." He says, his teeth gritted.

The question "Why does it matter." Mom makes an effort to upset him with her question.

"Reply to the inquiry." He claims that he is becoming angrier and granting moms' wishes. She twitches her lip, and I can tell that she's trying not to laugh. Just happy I figured out how to school my face.

"You respond to mine." My mum remarks while feigning a small smile.

"Dang it women, I asked you first, and I'm an Alpha." Trying to pull that card, he claims.

Even if you are an alpha, you are not mine. She says, and I notice a very little flinch on his part. Mom's eyes flickered with pity at the same instant he flinches, but they both vanish before the naked eye could detect them.

Why must you be such obstinate women. He says, moving closer to her and yelling a little bit with a growl in his voice.

Never mention my mum in such a way, please. I say, moving in front of them and raising my voice to a roar. I may have grown weary of their immature bickering, but no one has the right to talk ill of my mother.

"So, she's your daughter." From behind me, he says, addressing my mother. "Who is the dad?"

The question "Why does it matter." My mum asks the same question as I said. Although we don't often talk in unison, when we do, it's unsettling. He lets out a frustrated groan before taking a big breath and continuing.

Do you even recognize the father? I snarl loudly in response to what he says.

"Her eyes have an interesting color, aren't they Cole?" My mother asks, obliquely responding to his query. His eyes are like mine in size and hue. He is unmistakably my father.

He gives me about two seconds of eye contact before huffing and bolting away. Mom indicates for the boys to depart once he leaves, and we enter the region. While we stroll the way to her father's house, Mom occasionally points out things, and although though she might never confess it, I can sense she missed home. The distance is less than anticipated, and soon we are approaching a two-story house.

The window seals and door are a strange shade of blue, and the home is an odd shade of yellow. It's a fascinating house, and based on the expression in my mother's eye, it has always been that way. Her eyes have a familiarity to them, but they also have a look of suffering. She was deeply hurt by her mother. She has told me this story numerous times. Now that her mother has fled, I have a feeling some of those memories will be replaced by more positive ones.

We approach the door and gently knock on it. A man no older than 35 opens the door in a matter of seconds, yet we werewolves age more slowly than humans.

"Ari? Who is that? He speaks with a strong baritone voice that nearly sounds teary. He is shocked to see her, and his eyes are glassed over with unshed tears.

"Andrew. It's nice to see you once more. Mom says while sporting a little smile.

Who is at the door, Andrew? Says a voice. This voice sounds a little older and more grizzled. That would be my granddad, at least, I can only guess that. I watch as a few tears trickle down my uncle's face as he cradles my mother in his arms and presses his face deep into her neck. Alpha Cole might become angry if he saw another man approaching a woman's neck right now. But given that he rejected her, I imagine he wouldn't care.

"Ari?" Now get very close, the somber voice commands. Mom withdraws from the hug she is giving her daughter so she can look her father in the eyes as he speaks in a somewhat teary tone.

"Hi dad." was all she managed to say before being dragged into another agonizing hug.

You never phoned to confirm, so I assumed you wouldn't show up and I wouldn't have the chance to apologize for everything I had you go through and I-I-I. He says while sobbing and stammering what he can.

"Shhhhh. Okay, dad. It's ok. I was unable to make a follow-up call. After obtaining clearance, we began arranging our arrival here. Mom explains that she used to rub my back when I was little and depressed.

"What do you mean by 'we'?" Andrew inquires before wiping his eyes and turning to face me. My unnamed grandfather glances up and recognizes me despite his tears. He sits up straight and wipes his eyes before giving me his full attention before turning to face my mother again.

Who might this be, you ask? He queries my mom.

My daughter is shown here. This is your uncle Andrew and your grandfather Marcus, Cassie. Cassie Mora is my strongest warrior in my pack and my pride and delight. Mom says with an expression of love and pride on her face. I find myself grinning at the expression on her face.

I am an uncle. Do you recognize the father? Without presumably considering how awful that sounds, Andrew asks his mother. Mom merely gives him a "really" expression. "I'm only now realizing how awful that sounds. Ari, I apologize; I'm just stunned. Our weren't even expecting when you left, after all. You were never a social person; instead, you were totally career-focused.

"You must have met your soul mate then." Says Marcus. "Is he also here?"

Most likely somewhere. The night before I left, he turned me down. Just before I was scheduled to leave for the study program, Stella disowned me the night before. I asked the alpha if I may move there permanently at that time because I had no reason to continue staying. After hearing everything, he concurred. Tomorrow, I want to go see him and tell him how much I appreciate everything he has ever done for me. Mom gives me a side hug after explaining. She has always found it difficult to explain this, and I have always served as a sort of lifeline for her.

"He's inside this pack?" Marcus asks with a shocked expression. You didn't need to return, honey. I wouldn't have invited you to come here if I had known. How come you didn't tell me?

"I've moved past it long ago. I was given a piece of the Luna above to help me get through the rejection. As she kisses my forehead, my mother says.

"Let's go inside, why don't we?" Says Andrew. We all nod in agreement and enter.

Alpha's Daughter Rejected: Chapter 6

Cassie's POV

The interior of the house is more finer and has obviously been occupied by guys. I'd say the two people in front of me. On the leather couches in the living area, we all take our seats.

"I apologize, Cassie. I've been incredibly rude. Tell us a little more about yourself, please. Introducing himself to me for the first time, my grandfather says. Not that I have anything against him; he's only just had his first encounter with his daughter in 18 years.

"I don't have anything noteworthy about me. I enjoy running, I'm our pack's strongest warrior, and I've been invited to instruct the Warriors of several packs, including the one where we will be staying while we are visiting. I say it plainly. Actually, there isn't much to say about me. I spend all of my time practicing defense, and I never let my guard down. I still stand with my feet shoulder width apart, my arms folded.

My mother says, "Always on guard," I hear her say. She also enjoys reading and will often spend a lot of time reading and relaxing by the pond close to our home. She is an excellent artist and, despite her denials, she adores kids.

"I have no problem stating that I love kids; it's simply risky to acknowledge that you appreciate being around somebody so helpless. especially if you have no means of defending your adversaries. I say as I address my mother.

You don't have any opponents who would dare to oppose you, much less harm the kids you frequently watch over. With a rolled-eye expression, my mother says.

So you frequently look after children? With a trace of wonder in his eyes, Andrew queries.

"Yes. In that way, I resemble my mother a lot. I speak while noticing a brief, millimeter-sized smile form on my lips.

The boys wouldn't let mom cook, so we spoke for the next three hours while ordering Chinese for lunch because we were all too busy to cook. We were laughing so hard at one point that I had to take a seat. I was able to unwind a little bit even though I was still on alert. Then, about twelve, a visitor showed up. Andrew got up to go and returned carrying a man who appeared to be older. He and Alpha Cole had a striking resemblance, therefore I can only assume they are related.

"Alpha, Jason?" Mom says and gets to her feet.

Ariya Mora. You were getting ready to depart for your exciting future when I last saw you. What are you doing in this neighborhood? With a cheesy grin, Jason says.

"Conditions have changed. I'm here for a few weeks to spend time with my family again. My mum has gone. Hugging her older alpha, she exclaims while doing so.

Did you take up the Luna's offer to find you a new partner then? From the embrace, he asks while staring down at her. His only expression is one of worry, but I presume that given his age, he has nothing to be concerned about.

"No. I came away with a piece of him, and I would have never been able to let go. I don't really want to, though. Mom says, walking over to me and grinning. The elder man glances at me for the first time, and a shocked expression appears on his face. He gives my eyes a long, glazed look that I can see.

I understand struggling to move on. What is this? He says, but it seems like he already knows the solution.

"Jason. Meet Cassie Mora, your grandchild. Mom says while having both happy and sad looks. It's a strange combination that makes me want to hug her, but I know she would rather I waited for now.

"Granddaughter?" My grandfather and uncle both inquire at the same moment.

Why didn't you inform them? Jason looks at my mother inquisitively and asks.

I didn't want them to despise their alpha because of a choice he made as a youngster. Mom says while shrugging.

"It was a choice that destroyed the life of my baby girl." Marcus says with rage.

He injured my sister, yes. I have a good cause to despise him. Andrew nods while displaying tremendous agitation.

"I concur that his choice was totally stupid." Jason speaks while displaying an excessive amount of agitation.

"Exactly for this reason, I didn't want to tell you guys. I've moved past that and have no regrets. The best thing I've ever had came to me on that one night. She is the only thing that got me through everything. Therefore, I don't despise him and I don't feel guilty. Mom exclaims proudly as she observes me.

Furthermore, both of you hurt her when she was a child in some way. When she was excommunicated that morning, did either of you attempt to stop her or defend her?They both look down in shame as I continue, and sadness can be seen in their eyes.

The question is, "Does he know?" Asks Jason.

He approached her this morning and indiscreetly inquired about her family. Her eyes clearly show that he is her father, and he is aware that I am her mother, but I'm not sure if he has completely recognized that she is his daughter. I anticipate hearing from him soon so that she can join us for a meeting. says my mother.

"So long as you've made an effort to alert him," With a worried expression on his face, Jason says.

Will I get to meet your partner? I query Jason. After losing one grandmother, I would like not to lose the other.

She was tragically attacked by rouges last month and has been unconscious ever since. He says while hiding a pained expression on his face.

"Oh no!" My mother shouts. How will Luna Angie fare?

Although she is currently stable, she is still recovering from a serious brain injury, so it will take some time. He says while softly grinning.

"Am I right in thinking I have her eyes?" Looking him in the eye, I ask.

"Yes. You possess my exquisite Angle'e eyes. I can only presume you acquired them from my son as he has them as well. Mom nods as he speaks. I'm sorry, love; I realize it must be difficult.

I don't consider them to be his eyes. I picture them as Luna Angie's eyes and my daughter's eyes. Mom says while shrugging.

Well, I have to leave. Too long have I been away from my Angel, and my wolf is starting to get restless. The prodigal daughter's return makes me happy. One day before you depart, we'll need to go out to lunch. We're the only three there.As he offers his arms for a hug, Jason adds. When mum has finished her hug, she leaps into his arms, and I step aside to shake his hand.

"It's about time we returned. As we had promised, we would return for dinner, even though it was some distance away. Observing the time, I say.

We all bid each other farewell before returning to the meeting spot. When we are three-quarters of the way to the meeting place, we see a grey blob go by us, and I can hear mom's breath catch in her throat. I phone the boys to tell them to meet us there. When we arrive at the meeting spot, the boys are not yet there.

Even though I know it's just my father, I nevertheless stand between my mother and him when we hear rustling in the bushes behind us.

"We should speak." As soon as he emerges from the bushes, he demands. He is simply sporting a pair of basketball shorts, and based on how stern his voice is, you can tell he has recently changed. I assist mom by answering for her and standing up so she can see less because I know it's difficult for her to maintain eye contact.

If you genuinely think the doctor in front of you needs to hear from you, please make an appointment so that she can respond to you as soon as possible. I speak in a monotone voice. My mother is touching my shoulder, and I recognize her touch.

We have nothing to discuss, Cole, unless you stop attempting to use that alpha tone on me. My mum says to advance.

She is standing between us and we have a very good reason to talk. literally, that is. He adds that final tidbit as an addition.

We won't meet again until you understand that the alpha tone will never work on me. As the boys arrive, she says. The boys climb out of the car as she turns around and walks to the back seat. I'm about to turn back when I hear him murmuring something.

The question "What was that?" I inquire as I watch him bow his head in humiliation.

"Please." As he says it, his voice crackles a little bit. I give him a nod and quickly look up to catch it.

I can see a flicker of relief in his eyes. I turn around, proceed to the car, get in, and we leave him behind as we drive away. Mom puts her head on my shoulder as I begin to reassuringly rub my hand through her hair. She shuts her eyes and quickly nods out. She's had a long day and is feeling too many different things. She merits the rest.

Alpha's Daughter Rejected: Chapter 7

Cassie's POV

When we return home, I carry mom inside and put her on her bed in the guest room. I set an alarm to wake her up in an hour so I can go to Axe's office and tell him everything that happened while we were gone.

"Hey. How was it? I may now enter, Axe adds as he opens the door wider. The Beta, Caspian, and Whiskey are already present.

"It went rather well. I can now say that my father, both of my grandfathers, and my uncle have all been presented to me. Thankfully, I didn't need to speak to my father too often. My grandfathers and uncles are people I've gotten to know fairly well, and they seem to be generally decent. We made a direct route to the house and then a direct route back, as we had arranged. There weren't any issues. However, I do need to discuss courteous dialogue with my father with my mother. Giving them a quick briefing, in my opinion.

Do you believe she will take the risk? Whiskey remarks brusquely, disliking the notion of his mother being unhappy.

"If I ask her, I believe she will comply. Whiskey, I wouldn't want to offend her either, but I also believe that he deserves the opportunity to speak with her about the matter. I say as I observe him. Despite the fact that Mom always gave me the option to meet him, now that he has, I want to give him the chance to comprehend why I kept away. I should at least give him a little chance to get to know me. "I'll tell you what. It might be the only opportunity he'll ever have. I'll wager the person coming with you tomorrow, and if your mother is okay with it, we'll meet him at a small cafe on my property so nobody from his pack gets a chance to poke their heads in where they shouldn't. I can ask the group to leave the cafe temporarily so that we can have a quiet discussion. He can come see me as an excuse, which will prevent more inquiries. Leaning back in his chair and placing his feet up on his desk, Axe speaks.

That is nice to hear. When mum awakens from her slumber, I will discuss the matter with her. Is there anything else you want to talk about? I ask.

"You claimed to have met your grandfathers, both of them. Do you mean to say that you also met your father's father? Axe asks, his eyebrows arched.

"Yes. He was the only person who was aware of my mother's rejection and the knowledge that my father was her mate, and he learned that she had returned to town. She didn't tell him until she was already in Oregon that she was pregnant, but then again, neither did she. He feels terrible about his son rejecting my mum. She was always liked by his family, and if she hadn't been turned down, they would have taken her in and let her to continue working as a doctor in the pack. I speak with a hint of melancholy in my voice as I consider what my mother had to endure.

"Your mother is a brave woman, my love. She has always been an extremely intelligent girl. She'll come out of this with the finest possible result. Always, she does. She's got you, I mean." Coming over to give me a hug, says Whiskey. I give him a shoulder smile.

"Laundry time for dinner, guys. Cassie, dear, your mother has awakened. She expresses gratitude for the alarm. When Cassandra knocks on the door, she says.

We'll be leaving in a moment. The rest of you may proceed to go. I simply want to discuss tomorrow's plans with these two. Clapping Axe and I on the shoulders, whiskey says.

Whiskey, please don't take too long. As he speaks, Caspian gives his spouse and partner a sweet kiss.

"I give no guarantees," Before the smile can be removed from his face, he says while grinning and shuts the door. "All right, kids. Sit." We both do, and our brows are arched. How long do you two intend to keep your relationship a secret?

The question "How'd You Know?" Asks Axe while leaning back in his chair.

"I am aware of what mates look like." But I am aware of the reality, says Whiskey.

"You overheard us talking one night." I say. Why are all the grownups here being such drama queens.

"Well, that's too." He shrugs and says.

"After things have cooled down. We'll inform folks when mum is more content with things. We're taking our time to get to know one another till then. I say outlining our situation.

Axe responds, "I agree."

Do you still kiss?" Whiskey looks between the two of us and asks.

Still not. Why?" Axe asks, his brows furrowed.

"If you two don't act quickly, your wolves will panic and begin pushing you two to. They'll take control eventually and at least kiss. It serves as a check to make sure you are not rejecting one another. Whiskey adds with a smile that he was glancing between the two of us.

You stated, 'at least kiss. Are you saying they might go further? I ask.

They refused to brand one another. They wouldn't be legally recognized as being together in Luna's eyes, at least not without human permission. says whisky.

"GUYS! Dinner is becoming chilly. When Cassandra yells up the stairs, we all get up and go downstairs for dinner.

Dinner proceeds relatively quietly and without much conversation. Everyone was so preoccupied with eating that, except from the odd compliments to the cook, they simply lost track of words. Most of us returned to the office after supper, and this time my mother joined us. We quickly summarized all that had been discussed prior to supper and informed mum of everything that had been said. The enjoyable part is now.

"Mom." She hums in return when I say something to capture her interest. "I believe we ought to talk to him. I believe you should give a reason for not telling him about me so that I may give you my reasons for not wanting him in my life. I never wanted him to be aware of my existence, but now that he knows, I don't believe it would be fair to keep me away from him without a justification.

"I am aware of your perspective. You can count on me, my darling. You must already have a plan, right?" I nod in response to her question before Axe takes the lead.

The idea is to invite him over to a little cafe we have in our group so that we can speak privately. No one will question their absence because secret meetings frequently take place there; therefore, they won't be bothered. As a result, his pack won't be able to interrogate him; instead, he can simply claim that he merely met with me to discuss things. As he speaks, Axe forms a steeple out of his fingers. What a Sherlockian move on his part.

"That would function. Tomorrow, I'll talk to him about it. If that works for you, we might perform it the next day. Both my mother and Axe concur.

I'll speak with him. I don't want you talking to him all the time. I could be open to giving him a shot, but I don't trust him. preferably with you. Until I have a chance to speak with dad privately, I say that I want to keep mum away from her.

"Ok. Just take care. I am aware that I am immune to his rage, but I am unsure of how he will react to you. My mother says, her expression displaying worry. Axe briefly gives me the impression of being worried, but he quickly hides it.

~

The meeting ended quickly since everyone was exhausted and went to bed right away. After an hour, I decided to wait for Axe in the living room. He arrived a minute later and was dressed as the stereotypical character he is in a pair of black basketball shorts and a white tank top.

With a smile on his face, he says, "Hey."

I introduce myself by grinning. I won't remain expressionless when I'm around him.

"So, quick question, how well do you know my grandfather?" After some while, he queries. I anticipated that the query will be raised at some point. Answering it is not a problem for me.

"My mom was seeking for work when I was little, possibly around 4 or 5. The pack doctor was not permitted to train anyone else because the pack was ruled by a separate alpha. I accompanied my mother when she went to your grandfather's pub to look for work since she didn't have anyone to babysit me and she trusted me because I was a well-behaved kid. I say with a chuckle and a half-smirk. Because it was late, my mother went to the rear to speak with the manager while I was still in my pajamas. After receiving a kiss on the forehead from my mother, I went to the bar, stepped up onto a stool that was far too big for me, and sat down next to Whiskey. He gave me this expression of complete perplexity and arched an eyebrow when I asked the bartender for a Dr. Pepper. What on earth is this child doing in a pub, they both seemed to be asking as they exchanged looks with one another. Once I had my Dr. Pepper, Whiskey asked me the same question. I addressed the fact that my mum was looking for employment and hoped to secure a position here. After a little bit more conversation, he took a brief break and returned not two minutes later. Apparently, after seeing how respectable my mom was, he went to speak with the boss and insisted that she receive the job. What follows is history. I explain while grinning.

Grandpa Whiskey is a fairly cool person, I guess. He never stops moving and managing his, er, business. Axe states without specifying what that company does.

"I'm aware he's a mafia boss. When I was eight, I learned and didn't care. Due to all that dad has done for us, Mom didn't either. I shrug and smile as I say. He nods in agreement while displaying an expression of wonder.

We continue to converse, but before I know it, it is time for us to go to bed because we both have things to do in the morning. He gives me a kiss on the tip of my nose as we say our goodnights, which makes me smile more than I'd like to admit. As he turns to walk away, I grab his arm, twist him around, and give him a jaw kiss. He gives me a little look of disbelief, but I gave him a smug grin and strode away, turning around to wink at him. Overall, I'd say that today was quite productive.

Alpha's Daughter Rejected: Chapter 8

Cassie's POV

"We need to speak." I say moving closer to my father.

As expected, Axe followed my mother and me to her father's place this morning. We lingered there for a bit until I left after saying I had a meeting to attend. I tracked my father to his office and persuaded his beta to let me speak with him during that meeting. I'm in my father's office now, telling him something that he needs to know.

"John, you may proceed. This gathering is personal. If there is anything we need, I'll call you in. As he waves the Beta off, he says. Dad puts down his pen and runs his hands over his face after John has left and is no longer audible. "What did she say?" you ask.

"She concurred. She, Alpha Axe, you, and I will be there. Tomorrow, we'll meet up in a small café on his territory. No one will wonder why the cafe is closed to the public because it is typically used for meetings, and no one from your pack will have to find out. You are welcome to bring whomever you like, but they will learn details about my mother and I. Additionally, I'd like to ask to meet with you the day following the meeting to go over a few topics. Laying everything out on the table quickly, I say.

"Everything looks feasible. Alpha Axe is omniscient? He inquires after a brief period of profound thought.

"He has been told. One of the conditions for us living with him was this. He doesn't criticize your choice, or at least he has stated he wouldn't need to till he heard why you made it. He wants to be there tomorrow in part because of this. He claims that his findings tomorrow won't have an impact on your peace agreements or financial resources. He wouldn't endanger the pack for a personal motive. He must be there in order for all of your justifications and defenses to hold water, which is another reason he will be there. I provide justifications for everything.

He nods and exhales deeply before gently exhaling. "Why do we have to meet the following day?" He looks up at me and asks, appearing perplexed.

"After everything, I have a lot of questions I need to ask you. You have the day tomorrow and I have the day after for inquiries. I make it clear.

"Why did she keep you away from me?" He asks, a hint of grief coming through in his voice.

"I made the choice. She was honest with me, and I made the decision. She was in great pain as she tried to inform you. She endured great anguish while attempting to tell you, I can tell you from personal experience. I experienced it a few times when I was still in the womb and a few more times when I was a little child and she neglected to seal the bond. It seems as though Luna up there forbade her from telling you. Zoning out, I say.

"Why would Luna keep you away from me?" He asks while dozing off and with a somewhat softer voice.

"Perhaps she believed that you two wouldn't be able to handle a child. Perhaps she want for you to mature independently. As we both sat there absolutely unfocused, I say. We remain in that position for at least a minute before my phone alerts me that I have a text. I was aware of what it was. Axe warned me not to be gone for too long and threatened to text me if I did. I gave him the side-eye and turned to leave, but I was aware that he would continue. And when I looked at my phone, I saw that I was correct.

"Alright. I must leave. The alpha recently joined us and wants me back.

"Ok. Then I'll see you tomorrow. To walk me out, he motions while standing.

"You'll do. You might wish to make a list of questions for tomorrow so that everything goes well. The number of questions you ask and their importance are irrelevant. I can't guarantee that we will answer every question, but everything we do will be answered honestly, whether it be the simplest or the most crucial in your life. I add getting up and moving toward the door. He gives me a nod before opening the door.

I return to my grandfather and uncle's home by foot, and the moment I open the door, Axe starts asking me questions.

What have you been doing? Why was it so long? Why did you not respond to my text? He fires repeatedly at me.

I was on my way back when I said, "I was telling my dad about the meeting, he had some questions, and if I'm completing the task I won't respond to the commander." I text my father to let him know that I returned. I usually text the person I just left to let them know I'm okay even though he might not be driving. When I was younger, my mother constantly made me do it.

"Honey! Who is that? From the living room, Mom yells.

"Yeah, mom!" Axe enters the room after me, I say.

"How was your meeting with Sweetie?" Mom smiles and asks. Marcus and Andrew both smile at her, clearly pleased to see her so joyful. Jason is also present, and when he sees my wife's eyes, he smiles and makes eye contact with me.

"It wasn't too bad. Everything is ready to go, and tomorrow is the big day. I speak while keeping my arms crossed and my feet shoulder-width apart.

"You sound like you're about to commit a hit," someone said. Jason chuckles as he says. I pause for a moment, and Andrew gives me a brow-raising look.

"You're not really committing a hit, are you?" He asks, his eyes wide. I find myself grinning and giggling heartily at him.

"No, I simply have another meeting scheduled for tomorrow, and mum needs to come with me, so we can't come over. Additionally, I have a few things to finish, so for a few days, it might just be my mother and a guard. I describe squinting at the three boys.

Alright, Sweet Heart. Just be certain to return before you depart. Grandpa Marcus remarks while grinning melancholy. All of their faces have it, as I can see. I am aware of their regret at having missed my formative years and their desire to make amends, but they are unaware that I won't be too far away.

I'll make certain to. I smile as I say.

I'm sorry to interrupt, but we must leave. A little uneasy, Axe admits. He has work to do, but he doesn't want to ruin the family gathering.

"Sure," you say. Grandpa Jason replies as he gets up to lead the group of us to the door. Omega Axe, Being with you once more was fantastic. I hope to see you ladies sometime this week, ladies. I must now depart because I need to speak with my son about some business.

After bidding each other farewell, we proceed to the location where the boys are supposed to meet us and find them waiting. Mom falls asleep on my shoulder during the largely quiet return trip in the van. Without my lack of complete comfort in the location, I probably would have fallen asleep too. Tonight I have to go on a wolf run. After returning to the pack home and getting mum inside, I once again put her down for a nap while going to the office to speak with Axe. Since there were only the two of us in his office, we were able to be a little more honest, but we still had to keep the conversation business-related.

What happened to you? He asks, inhaling deeply and exhaling with a sigh.

"I traveled to tell my father about the meeting. I stayed longer than I had anticipated because he ended up asking a few questions. I'd never tell you the truth. I'm telling you that I have a second appointment with him the day after tomorrow because of this. I say. Truth-omission is still unacceptable in my book.

"Why? I hoped we might schedule some time to hang out. He adds, whimpering a little in jest and giving me a pout that quickly turns into a smile.

"I was hoping too, but I have a few questions for him, and I want tomorrow to be about him getting answers," she said. I truly say that. He will always be someone I can trust and relax with.

"What did I do to earn your favor? I must have had a previous life as a saint. He finally speaks after gazing at me for a while.

What did you do to deserve someone as nasty as me, I was wondering? I laugh as I say.

"Would you kindly assure me that you don't really feel bad about yourself?" He queries. He scoffs and gives me an oddly triangular look when I don't respond. I've only known you for three days, yet you're already one of the best individuals I know.

"Perhaps that is the issue."

"In the three days I've known you, you've taken care of your mother as if you were the mother, you've done everything you can to help out around the house, despite the fact that you're just a visitor, you've handled the kids like nobody's watching, and you've shown that you're a fantastic Luna," the man said. Do you know how difficult it was for me to hold back my feelings of love for you in those moments after your mother spent an hour talking about how wonderful you are, how much she loves you, and all you've ever accomplished? I am aware of information that your mother shared with me that I doubt you would have shared. She informed me about numerous actions you took when you were younger that came naturally to you. You are a lovely person, and if given the chance, you will make a wonderful Luna. So, sure, how did I earn your favor? What did I do to earn the presence of the most incredible woman to ever walk the earth? With each statement, he stands up and moves in my direction. When he's done, he'll be standing in front of me and will be cocking his head to look me in the eye.

I can't help but lean forward after a speech like that. He stares at me in awe before turning to look at my lips. He has trouble breathing, and I know I do too. He pauses before speaking and turns to stare back into my eyes.

"May I?"

"Please." Without a second's hesitation, I state.

Not a second later, I feel something warm and soft against my lips. When I feel his palm on my cheek, I apply a little more pressure and can't help but close my eyes. I open my eyes to find the most stunning eyes I've ever seen as he pulls away.

"Wow." He says before laughing briefly. I grinned and let out a small chuckle of my own.

"Wow, definitely." I declare while beaming like the cat who caught the canary.

A knock at the door, along with a beaming Whiskey, separates us.

"Congratulations." He declares with eyes shining with delight.

The question "How'd You Know?" Have you taken a step back? Axe queries. He's now leaned on this desk as though we were simply having a conversation.

Even in the smallest things, consent. I quote in time with the whiskey. I wink at Whiskey as he turns to smile at me. HE says, "Wolf hearing," and points to his ears. The meal is ready.

The rest of the evening consists of a relaxed meal, a quick run around his pack, and then it's time for bed. I'm relieved that everything went smoothly because tomorrow will be more difficult and I worry about mom. I don't meet Axe that evening. As we sleep during the night, I have dreams about the kiss. I smile as I go off to sleep.

Alpha's Daughter Rejected: Chapter 9

C ole's POV

It's unbelievable that I have a daughter. I've only ever slept with one person, Ari, and I was inebriated. I hardly recall it, and now I am a mother of a daughter. And she's really tough. She needed to acquire that somewhere. When we were younger, I didn't really talk to her mother, but if she was anything like she is today, she was a pill. Why did I even turn her down?

I have a ton of questions about her and about them both. I'm so happy Cassie persuaded Ari to let me speak with her. The fact that Cassie respected her mother enough to ask is already better than anything I've ever done, though I doubt she would have if she had wanted to.

And it says so much about her character that she personally broke the news to me and provided me specifics. She's way older than she ought to be. Ari was fiercely discussing all the things she has done when my dad butted me with a phone call. The two of them obviously take care of one another the way a mother and daughter should. While I'm happy for her, I'm also sorry I couldn't be there for it all.

Regarding not knowing about her, I'm not sure how I feel. If Cassie's claims are accurate, I guess I get it. She may have been taught not to reveal any dishonesty, or it may simply be what she sincerely thinks, but I didn't detect any on her part. I suppose I can understand why she wouldn't want to meet with me, but she ought to have informed me.

No, she was unable to. You would have insisted on seeing her, which would have undermined the whole point of her decision. My wolf informs me.

Okay, that seems sense, but would it be improper for me to be interested in my child?

When did you behave as you did? Yes.

I may have been wrong to reject her mother, but I can't even recall doing it.

You don't, of course; that happened 18 years ago. You also had a hangover.

Okay, does it hurt you to be around her? Why are you making fun of me?

It does, of course. You foolishly shattered the connection, and I'm sure it hurts her as well. She's probably the only one left alive thanks to Cassie.

Why shouldn't Cassie be the only thing keeping her alive?

because a piece of us is still with her. We weren't all lost to her. We are a part of Cassie. It stands to reason that Luna would not permit her to tell you. If she refused to see you, you would demand your daughter and take the only thing that was keeping her alive. You would come storming around, hurting her.

I wouldn't have carried that out!

In your early years, you were a dick. You certainly would.

Okay, so perhaps I would have—no qualifiers. After what you did to our mate, you had no right to her. In the human world, you might have rights to her, but those laws don't apply to us. We have Wolf Laws because of this.

Did you just break off our connection? You're so rude, you're a buttface!

"Alpha? Are you okay? Since that female departed, you've been dozing off. My beta yells in my face, saying.

"Yeah. I'm just a little anxious. Tomorrow, I have a meeting at the North Carolina pack. If I can keep my father away from my mother for a long enough period of time, I'll probably take him along, but if not, you can stay in her room and watch after her. Getting down to business, I declare. My father is acceptable to come because he is already aware of my daughter.

"The girl that was here will return the following day to follow up on the meeting.

"Good job, boss. Then I'll bring her right up. He says while giving his head a nod.

"Thanks, dude. Please send my father over.

Yes, sir. I'll immediately send him over. Does anything else?

Who asked, "What's for dinner?" I ask while famished.

"Tacos."

"Yessssssss!" Suddenly aroused, I respond. He gives me the evil eye for being rude and proceeds to look for my father.

My father arrives quickly, complaining that he hasn't seen my mother in too long as he settles down on the comfortable couch in my office.

"Father. Stop whining; I'll get you back to her right away.

"What is it, son?" He asks as he settles in and makes himself comfortable.

Before I reply, I can't help but roll my eyes.

"Ari and Cassie have scheduled a meeting for us to meet tomorrow so I can get to know them. I needed to know whether you would accompany me so that it would appear that we were actually discussing pack business. You'll have the opportunity to get to know your granddaughter as well.

I recently returned from Ari's father's residence. I know more about Cassie than you do since she talks a lot about her. I am certain of that. Rolling his eyes, he says.

I ask, evidently annoyed, "Do you want to go or not, old man?"

"Are you aware that screwing with Ari was a mistake?" He asks, his face furrowed.

"Yes. Not only did I miss Cassie's development, but I also regret it. Now respond to my query.

Yes, I'll leave. But you must assign someone to watch over your mother. If she awakens, please let me know. What time and where is this meeting now?

"At the NC pack tomorrow. They will pick us up at the border meeting location and take us to this small cafe where they hold meetings. I tell him as I snap my neck because the stress has returned.

"Well then," he says, getting to his feet and stretching, "I'm going to go see your mother and chat to her for a little while. I'll see you in the morning.

I lay back and close my eyes as I take it all in as he nods to me before leaving. I'm terrified as hell since I have no idea how this is going to happen, but I'm also eager to meet my daughter. She set up this meeting with her mother, which I owe her. I don't know how I'm going to pay her back.

Alpha's Daughter Rejected: Chapter 10

Cassie's POV

For the first time in 17 years, my mother and father really had a conversation today. My mum is making me anxious. I've informed her that she needs to let me know if being around him is causing her undue suffering so that we can take a break. While mom appears cool, I know she's panicking out as we wait for the lads to pick up Cole. Every now and then, I hear her heartbeat quicken and see her take a deep breath, indicating that she has probably been thinking of Cole.

It won't take us very long to wait. Cole shows up and takes a seat next to my mum. My mother was surprised to see him bring his father around, and she grinned. Cole must also be smitten by the smile on my mother's face because I notice a very small intake of breath.

"Shall we get started?"Cole opined.

"We'll do. Have you got any queries? My mum says while addressing him directly. She does this out of complete respect rather than out of any ill will. She frequently lowers her head, yet I can tell that she is happy to be able to meet someone's eyes.

"Why did you keep her hidden from me." He asks more questions than he demands, which makes me frown at him. He winces and acknowledges the look, but his mother responds as if she hadn't heard him.

I tried. several times. Every time I attempted to, a sharp ache erupted inside of me. I was unable to move for the next two hours. Following the incident, I saw the doctor twice. They saw the pains but were unable to determine what was causing them. I once experienced that while pregnant and I made sure not to have it again. After having Cassie, I gave it another go, but this time the agony was much severe. I tried to ignore it, but it became so awful that I had to visit the hospital once. I knew it happened when I tried to tell you, and the Luna repeatedly verified it in my own dreams and in the dreams of many other people. Attempting to contract you was what caused the anguish. I have to consider my kid. I wanted to tell you so badly. Every couple of years, I tried again until Cassie was old enough to understand, at which point I gave her the choice. My mother clarifies. She mentions the pangs as she glances down. She told me a few years ago when I had the aches once more after waking up from a nightmare.

"Cassie." To catch my attention, he says. Why didn't you want to know about me?

Don't try to speak to me in an Alpha tone. You ask it in the form of a question if you want me to respond. With a little growl in my voice, I say.

'Nice.' Mom's snort may be heard in my head. She, Grandpa, and Axe are all beaming with pride, although I'm not sure if they all noticed Axe's outburst. Please explain why you kept it a secret from me. After a little pause, he asks. He seems to be taking satisfaction in the fact that I'm not a submissive, and I can sense it.

"You injured my mom. I was mature enough to make decisions by the time I was also old enough to comprehend the mate bond and the repercussions of rejection. I didn't want you near my mother since I knew how my mother would react to being around you. She informed me that you didn't know too much about her, and I believed it would be unfair to judge someone before getting to know them. I reasoned that you wouldn't want me if you didn't want my mother. I resemble her a lot. When I was younger, I didn't want you around for a variety of reasons. I say.

"You rejected me before you even knew me." With a wince tugging at his lips, he says.

"I was 6. What's your apologies? I say. Grandpa gives me a high five, Axe snorts, and mom smiles at me for this.

"I was a fool,"

"Was?" I say while acting shocked and raising my brows. Axe gives another high five and smiles, but this time he starts to chuckle inaudibly. Cole is clearly frustrated, and it's obvious to me.

"Cole." My Mother, he responds, turning his head in her direction. Do you have any more queries?

"Do you have any photos of your baby?" He queries. Mom grinned and took a little box out of her purse.

"When she was a baby, we didn't have many opportunities to shoot pictures. But she was quite attractive in photos. Mom chuckles and says with a little smile.

"Her favorite onesies are some of these, to name a few. When she was younger, she was an excellent archer and liked the sport. Her hair color changed frequently and was pretty peculiar. It became a little bit brighter as she grew older, and in the summer it was all over the area. She rarely wore dresses, so I grabbed all the photos of her that showed her wearing one. Mom explains while giggling.

"I maintain that. Regardless of what Disney says, they are incredibly impractical because you cannot effectively shoot a bow while wearing a tight dress. Even if the garment tears, your chances of getting an accurate shot are quite limited since your muscles are too constrained. I say, getting a little agitated.

What if you plan to attend a club? Grandpa queries.

Then what I just said holds true. In a dress, you can't properly sit down. At least without showing your underpants to the entire club. It would be better to wear jeans or another style of pant. I say. Furthermore, why would I dress up to go to a club? Who am I attempting to win over here? a chance encounter with a stranger I'll probably never see again? Why do they behave that way?

But what if you run into your soul mate? Grandpa challenges me by asking.

"I'm sure my friend wouldn't want me flashing anyone or wearing something so tight and revealing that it leaves nothing to the viewer's imagination if we met in a club," he said. Rolling my eyes, I say. The room was filled with a chorus of "he wouldn't"s.

I acknowledge that he wouldn't want that, but your recent outburst is the loudest I've ever heard you. I enjoy listening to you speak. With a smile on his face, he says.

"Have you actually ever been to a club?" Cole queries.

"Yes. several hundreds of times. I shrug and say.

"Why?! You're only seventeen; you ought to be familiar with a club's interior. He practically yells.

Cole, remain calm. As security at one, I work. I make sure that no fights start and, if they do, that they end quickly. I shrug and say.

Why are you required to work? I assumed that since your mother is the pack doctor, you are taken care of in every way. Grandpa queries.

"I often feel bored. I left school early, and training all day gets monotonous and unhealthy after a time. I reasoned that I might as well provide assistance.

~

I don't say much during the course of their two hours of conversation, speaking up only to respond directly to questions. Grandpa eventually got up and left after Cole and Mom had spent a lot of time talking and getting to know one another better. Grandma apparently came out of her coma, and he had to go get her. I appreciate him coming over to spend some time with my mother and I. They continued talking for another thirty minutes after he left before Cole had to return to his pack. When we returned to the pack home, I received a text message informing me that I was wanted to attend a battle that was taking place nearby. I sat down with my mother to discuss when I had a few hours.

"How are you doing, mom?"

"I feel awful."

We could have left if you had told us to. I might have thought of an explanation to get us out of there.

"No, child. That's not the reason I feel awful.

Why then, mom?

"I feel awful because I felt satisfied. being together and just exchanging words. Just so serene was my wolf. That shouldn't be how I feel. I ought to have been in pain. I ought to have been angry. I shouldn't have been satisfied at all. I simply want to spend more time with him. Why?" She cradles her head in her hands as tears start to spill from her eyes.

"Mom. Every event has a purpose. I'm unable to explain how Luna came to be this way. Would you rather spend the remainder of the journey apart from him?

"What will happen over the following few days is impossible to foresee. It could be necessary to meet with him. All I can do is survive.

I won't oppose as long as you commit to genuinely live. I smile as I say.

Hey, I'll leave before dinner and come back about midnight because I have a "meeting" in town later tonight.

"All right baby girl, just be cautious." She says, standing up to give me a forehead kiss before bending down to talk to the others.

I inform his mother and Axe before leaving for my fight.

Alpha's Daughter Rejected: Chapter 11

Cassie's POV

I managed to arrive at the subterranean pub where the fight would take place in a rented car and with plenty of time to spare. I had plenty of time to warm up and put on my regular clothes because of this. The previously described outfit comprises of a sports bra, shorts, a loose-fitting hooded tank top, and a straightforward pair of purple sneakers. Every time I had a fight, my trainer had essentially required that I wear this. My sole suggestion was that my hair needed to be pulled back into a tight ponytail because I didn't personally care.

I arrived without knowing much about my competitor other than their name, thus I was unable to formulate a strategy. This is standard practice for situations like this and is terrible. I've always been the type of person who requires a plan, but I've put too much in this to back out at this point. The moniker of my rival is "White Tiger," which I find absurd, but whatever, dude. Just "C" will do for me. I'm not really sure why you chose an animal for your name.

Even though it's not really necessary, my coach made the special trip out here to be here for this bout. Warm-ups don't take very long. I soon receive a call to the stage. "White Tiger" is standing across the ring from me and has already been called out. She is a 5'9" girl who is quite muscular and clearly has advanced this far from muscle alone. I can definitely move a little quicker than her because I'm smaller. I haven't seen her fight, so I can't judge how quick-witted she was.

The referee briefly discusses the regulations before telling the players to start, which are basically 1: No concealed weapons and 2: Avoid death. I get thrown over her shoulder as she charges at me while bending over at the waist. She dashes into the ropes when I sidestep her and then turns around. She gives me a somewhat more enraged face as she glances at me. She therefore has a short fuse. Once more, she charges in my direction, but this time I move to the side and extend my arm to clothesline her. She clutches me as she descends, and I actually feel my shoulder pop, but it works. It was probably audible throughout the entire space.

She is still lying down but is extremely close to standing up when I pop my shoulder and get up. I swiftly reach for her arm, lift her up, and then ram my head into hers. Despite the fact that it only slightly throws me off, she suffers much more consequences than I do because of the fall. I punch her hard in the gut, sending her doubling over and gasping for air as she tries to calm herself once again. After a brief pause for breath, she stands up straight once more. Despite the fact that she is still not feeling well from the head injuries and lack of oxygen in her lungs, she still tries to attack. Her eyes are still dilation.

She tries to punch me, nearly hitting me right in the jaw, but I manage to escape it just in time, sparing me a slight jaw nick. There will be a small bruise there for a short while, but it will disappear before I return home. In order to cripple her without breaking a bone, I grasp her hand before it passes too far over my head. She attempts to punch with her non-dominant hand while sucking air through her teeth, but because she hasn't had much practice using that hand, the punch is extremely sloppy and simple to block.

I roundhouse kick her and hit her in the head with it. She is defeated by this, which concludes the fight. When the referee checks on her, I make sure she doesn't have a concussion by checking her pulse, any additional wounds, and her pupils. I check to see if my opponent has suffered any severe injuries before changing and leaving for home.

~

I get up earlier than normal the following morning and go for a run. I have a little jaw ache and a sore shoulder, but I'll make it. I joined everyone for breakfast after my jog through the woods, and then my mother and I went into town. My mother stayed with the beta as my sister and I strolled to the Coles office, where we would have our private appointment. When I approach the beta of Cole's pack, he walks me right up to Cole's office. I am dropped off at the door, knock, and am welcomed inside right away.

"Cassie. Therefore, if yesterday was my day, today is when you should ask me questions. What then are they? As I settle into the chair across from him, he inquires.

"There's really only one question," I say and wait for his direction to continue. After some time, he finally instructs me to "shoot." Would you accept my rejection today if I gave it to you again?

Why would you pose an impossible question. I most certainly don't deserve such a thing, and the only person who could do it would be the Luna. He says, his voice dripping with regret.

Not at all what I asked for. I questioned if you would be willing to retract your rejection in the present. I just quoted myself, in fact. I say.

"It would be irrelevant. I could never be accepted by your mother. I don't blame her at all. he claims. He's pouting, that much is clear.

"Reply to Cole's inquiry. Would you accept a second opportunity at starting a family and getting your companion back? I say, no longer posing the sentence as a question.

"Yes. 1,000,000 times. He shakes his head and continues, "I can't help but think that I was such an idiot that I would lose everything." Just as someone is about to knock on the door, he abruptly leaps to his feet and sprints to the door, opens it quickly. He moves inside the doorway and shuts it, hiding me within. I lift an eyebrow at his back to ask a question, but a very irate female voice swiftly responds to my silent inquiry.

"YOU DISQUALIFIED YOUR MATÉ? WHAT GOT INTO YOU? You were raised better than that by me. 'Says' the woman.

Calm down, mom. You've just emerged from a two-month coma. You should take a nap. Cole says, attempting to pacify the women. Telling a woman to calm down is one thing you should never do, though.

"DID YOU JUST tell me to relax? AFTER LEARNING THAT MY SON DID ONE THING THAT IS CALLED THE WORST THING YOU COULD EVER DO, YOU EXPECT ME TO CALML ME DOWN? And now I discover that you are obviously attempting to hide the random woman you have in your office. She yells incessantly. She then storms the room, followed by Grandpa who looks like a lost dog.

"Hey, Grandpa." I say jokingly while grinning.

Hello, Sweetheart. You had a meeting today, didn't you? He says while arching his brow.

"I'm at my appointment. I wanted to ask him a few questions yesterday but was unable to.

"Pardon me! You are who?" I believe my mother asked Angie this question.

"Cassie Mora is my name." I say formally introducing myself to the woman who isn't yet aware that she is my grandmother.

It says, "This is our granddaughter." By placing a hand on her shoulder, my grandfather says.

AFTER REJECTING YOUR MATE, YOU WENT AND GOT A GIRL PREGNANT? She yells and approaches her son to slap him.

Actually, "it was before." I smile as I say. He gives me a look and mutters, "Not helping," at me. This only makes me grin more.

You previously had someone pregnant? DO YOU REJECT YOUR MATE FOR THAT REASON? She yells and strikes him once more.

"Cassie, I don't really like you right now." He says, raising his hands in an effort to deflect his mother's blows.

"You're receiving the punishment you deserved for rejecting my mother. Take this as my retaliation. I shrug and say.

"Honey, take a breath. Although what he did was wrong, Ari has pardoned him and given the go-ahead for him to meet Cassie. He says, not really explaining himself very well.

"His partner is my mum. They met at a party, had sex, and were together. He rejected her the following morning. When her mother rejected her and she was already on the road, she decided to relocate permanently. Her mother had moved away, and her father wanted to reestablish contact with her, so we recently returned. I was unknown to everyone. The moon goddess forbade her from telling your son since she left before she could do so. He's worked really hard to get to know my mother and me ever since he found out I existed. You should be proud of him for trying to make amends for his error. I say, fully outlining the circumstance.

Is Ari Mora really your mother? With tears in her eyes, she asks.

"Yes. Amazingly, my mother tried everything in her power to raise me. When I was old enough to understand, Mom gave me the option after trying her best to tell your son that he had a daughter but failing. I am equally at fault because I decided not to disclose. I reply, "I get it, kid. So, Cassie, was it, then? I'm glad to have met you. I'm Angie, and I suppose that makes me your grandmother. She adds while grinning and holding out her hand.

I'm glad to have met you, Angie. Cassie here. I say as I shake your hand and smile of my own.

How have you two never met despite being so similar to one another? Grandpa asks with a bewildered expression. Cole has a matching one. I look back at her after we both roll our eyes.

"If you want to talk to my mother, she's at her parents' place right now. The past few days have been spent chatting to her father and brother.

"That's fantastic. They should reconnect and get to know one another. Where do you reside? She asks while assuming a very professional businesswoman's appearance.

"We're residing at the close-by pack. We weren't supposed to get too near to Cole since our alpha didn't want it to harm. Even though Mom would have gone without his consent, it was just easier to acknowledge that this was the only way he would allow us to leave. I say with a shrug and a similar tone in my voice.

"Your mother was always the type to get what she wanted." She chuckles as she speaks. Before they continue on their journey, we converse for another minute. After completing my purpose for being here, I bid Cole farewell and leave. I then go back to the car to help my friends pack.

Alpha's Daughter Rejected: Chapter 12

Cassie's POV

Oh, how I miss Axe. When I ended my appointment with Cole and returned to the pack house, the first thing I did was go to his office because he had pack business and had to stay behind today. I knocked, and when I entered, I noticed him sitting with his pack doctor discussing some of the members who will require care following their training today.

I knew exactly who I needed to talk to. Here is our pack doctor, Remiro, for Cassie. This is Cassie, Remiro. For the remainder of her stay, she will be instructing the pack members. Cassie, I didn't anticipate your return so soon. What can I do to assist you with? preserving professionalism, he says. It wasn't lost on anyone that he called the pack "our" pack, but to the good doctor, it most likely sounded like he was referring to the pack as a whole or perhaps to both of them.

"My meeting ended sooner than anticipated, so I wanted to find out when you wanted me to begin my training. If you'd like, I can return later. In my professional voice, I use the word monotonous.

Oh no, the job is almost done. Therefore, Alpha, I'll need medical information for every adolescent trainee so that I'll know what to provide them if they become hurt. The ideal approach to do it would be to require all parents to complete a form with information on allergies and other considerations and return it to you before their child can start training. Doc remarks as he surveys the Alpha.

That sounds fantastic! Everyone should receive a mindlink. Young and old, I want updated files on everyone. When were our medical file updates last made? Asks Axe.

It was "two years ago."

"Well then, man, hop to it!" Axe makes a loud exclamation. Doctor nods before leaving.

He gets up and approaches me after an awkward minute and a half of silence. I extend my arms for a hug, and eh comes over and gives it to me without hesitation. He steps back, turns to face me, and begs for a kiss.

"Sure, that. I always give you the go-ahead. He slants forward to kiss me as I speak. I'm already dependent on him because of his velvety lips. He pulls back too quickly for me, but he's out of breath by then. I inhale deeply and turn to see the eyes I've already found love with.

"You are the most gorgeous person I have ever seen," someone said. He remarks with wonder in his eyes.

"And you are the most attractive." expressing to him the same awe, I say.

I was so sorry I missed you last night. I had trouble falling asleep. I ultimately stayed up until I heard you enter. I was tempted to check on you but refrained out of respect for you and believed you would be exhausted. He says, almost ashamedly, looking down.

"You ought to have arrived. I really wanted to see you. I was sorry I couldn't join in on our nightly talk. It seemed strange to try to go asleep without seeing you because I've grown accustomed to it. I say and take a seat.

Could you tell me what you had to do? He adds as he takes a seat on the couch in his office right next to me.

"I shouldn't tell you, but I'd rather you were aware. I had a fight last night as an underground fighter. There is now no way for me to escape because I have been in it for a very long time. Without a good reason, it would be absurdly difficult for me to leave. I shrug and add as I cling to his arm as he wraps it around me.

What do they consider to be a "valid reason"? He asks, his face furrowed.

"Pregnancy, union, or significant injury." I propose organizing them by frequency.

"I adore the order you put pregnancy and marriage." He chuckles as he speaks.

Because more want to 'enjoy' themselves after a quarrel, it's more typical for an underground women to become pregnant before getting married. Additionally, it happens frequently for warriors to marry one another and continue battling. A significant injury will frequently only temporarily halt them while they recuperate, after which they will resume fighting. I say elaborating on the solutions.

"Well, then." With furrowed brows and a shrug, he says. "Do you want children at all?"

"Yes. Many. My mother didn't want a second chance partner, therefore I would never be able to have a sibling, despite my desire for one. I don't want my children to grow up feeling isolated. I recall how lonely it was when there weren't many kids in the pack when I was a kid. The packs were pretty lonely at the time for a child my age because we were rotating Alphas, but now that we have settled in, there are many kids.

How many children would you like? He queries.

I chuckle and utterly jokingly respond, "7."

"Oh no, please. That's excessive. When he says this, his eyes swell up and he feels his head fall back. Truthfully, the idea doesn't appeal because having a child seven times doesn't sound enjoyable.

Yes, I was kidding. If I had to give birth that many times, I couldn't. Shaking my head, I say.

Which genders would you prefer? He replies as he starts stroking my hair with his fingertips.

"Two girls and three boys. The boys would be the girl's protectors, and because her brothers wouldn't let her not know how, the girl would be able to defend herself. We wouldn't have to worry about her being alone if something were to happen to us. That has always been my mother's main worry. She made sure that I would go to my father if something were to happen to her. Even better, she had a letter ready and let me know where to find it so I could have it before I was taken away. She had thought of everything. She showed your grandfather where the letter was, and he nearly tore it up. He claimed that "That no good piece o waste" would not succeed in taking his little D.P. No way, not at all. I recall how adamant the old man was that I was to remain his princess and that no one would be able to sever our relationship as I say with a chuckle.

"Yep, that sounds just like the old man." I lean closer to him while he speaks and yawns. We could take a quick snooze, you know. We could definitely get away with a 30-minute snooze if you tell your mom that you made it back—which I already had—and I tell the boys that I'm at a meeting. His eyes clearly showed how exhausted he was as he spoke while staring down at me.

So we actually did that. simply taking in the sensation of each other's arms.

Alpha's Daughter Rejected: Chapter 13

Cassie's POV

Training has begun. I wake up really early since I have been dormant for far too long and am ready to start this thing. We won't be going too extreme today, so I don a tank top and a pair of men's basketball shorts before heading over to the practice area. It's three in the morning, so it's hardly surprising that nobody else is there when I arrive. I perform my warm-up exercises, which include two miles of running, 150 push-ups, and 150 pull-ups, before taking a break to hydrate and wait for the others. Everyone who will be training today shows up on time at 5 a.m. Some of the older girls, who are around 16, are wearing sports bras that are too tight and virtually see-through leggings. All of the lads who are either the same age as the girls or one year older are staring at them, some with contempt and some with passion. Everyone looks rapidly to the field where they can see me, and a conversation breaks out.

"She's hot," "I thought the best warrior their pack had was gonna be here," "Where is he?" Among the words I hear flitting about the group are a few. Axe must have heard the last one as well because he bristles slightly at the remark before requesting silence.

"This is the Risen Moon pack of Oregon's finest warrior. You will treat Cassie Mora with the utmost respect, please. As if she were the moon goddess herself, you'll obey her commands. Any of you who disrespected her will be punished if I find out. We want to leave a good impression on her because she is a visitor. He says to everyone while furrowing his brow. He gives me a nod before leaving.

"First of all! You will immediately change if you are wearing something that is too tight or see-through. YOU WILL MISS THE INTRODUCTIONS, BUT WE CANNOT PROCEED WITHOUT YOU. I don't mind working out in sports bras and leggings, but I want them to fit right or be covered by a T-shirt. I speak louder so that everyone in the audience can hear me. I instruct everyone else to take a seat on the grass while a sizable group of girls and a few guys go to change. My group today is coed and ranges in age from 11 to 17. I'll have to divide them into categories as a result.

"I'm giving you the chance to ask me questions before we start our training because I know that trust isn't something that comes easily. While we wait for your peers, I want to win your respect so you can ask me anything. However, I will forewarn you that I might provide a brief response. As soon as I say it, everyone in the group raises their hands. I decide to go first with one of the younger girls.

Age: "How old are you?" The pigtail-clad 11-year-old girl inquires.

"I am 17. In a month and a half, I turn 18. I remark while indicating one of the elder boys.

"Have you found your soul mate?" The boy inquires, appearing to suggest that he might be my partner by wiggling his eyebrows.

"Yes." Without missing the disappointed expression on the prior boy's face, I say and gesture to the subsequent child.

Why don't you respond? Before hesitantly continuing, he pauses for a few period and turns to face the smaller children. "...completed the procedure?"

"I want to be able to offer him my complete attention, but I'm now quite busy. I'm hoping things will settle down soon so I can. I give a small youngster my explanation as I point toward him.

Why did you force them to change, you ask? He asks while wagging his head in confusion.

"What we're going to be doing today is not appropriate for what they were wearing, and it would be uncomfortable for them. Better for them to go change. I comment as I see the final set of girls leave in much more appropriate attire. "All right, gentlemen, let's get started. ten circuits around the field first, then anything else. You can take a two-minute break if you find it difficult to breathe, get some water (I'll have the Beta bring out a jug), and then return to your work if necessary. GO!" Thus, it starts.

~

The more seasoned individuals follow the younger ones, and our session is a little shorter than the others. Cassandra doesn't want to cook, so once I finish, we all go out to supper. My mother arrives back in time to catch the final session of the day. Thankfully, the setting wasn't really upscale because I'm against wearing a dress. That evening, my mother and I spend time in her room talking about the things she learnt about her father and brother today. She's thrilled to meet the real them and is really pleased about everything, but around halfway through our chat, she pauses and takes a trembling breath.

You know I adore you, right? She pauses for a moment to take a second breath before continuing. "This doesn't hurt physically. Being near him was supposed to hurt me physically, yet all I felt was satisfaction. When it was just the three of us, I couldn't help but be happy that we were a family. Since I've been apart from him, all I can feel is emotional misery. I don't know why; I acknowledged his rejection, but now it's as if nothing ever occurred. I don't understand, Cassie. She says as she envelops me in her arms. She sobs while burying her face in the crook of my neck.

I can only envelop her in my arms and watch her scream. My mother despises being in the dark, especially when it involves our life. Although I am equally perplexed, all I can think to do is turn to the Luna for guidance. I glance toward the moon and think of the goddess as my mother slumbers in my arms.

Give me advice so I can support my mum. I lay my mother down on her bed, think, and then close my eyes.

When I enter the living room, my partner is observing the gas fireplace, which is on for some reason. He appears to be deeply contemplative and is holding a glass of iced tea. He has a good scruff going on and hasn't shaved in a few days, which I adore. I approach him and take a seat next to him, resting my head on his shoulder. He places a kiss on top of my head while leaning his cheek on it, remaining completely focused.

How soon do you think we'll be able to inform everyone? He asks while stroking my head with his scruff.

"Hopefully soon. I desire to be able to kiss you in public. With the exception of a minor disagreement between my mother and father, I believe that most of the problems have been settled. But that will mostly depend on Luna. I add a little extra cuddling up next to him.

He turns to face me and says, "Speaking if kissing--" he can now see my face."- may I?"

"Sure," you say. I speak, and without pausing, our lips come together. And spending the evening in such manner was ideal. giggling when with my partner.

Alpha's Daughter Rejected: Chapter 14

Cassie's POV

I was lying on my partner when I suddenly found myself in a grassy meadow under a stunning night sky. The voice that emerged was much more angelic, despite the fact that it was incredibly wonderful.

"Hello, child." The speaker's voice sounds like it is coming from a surround sound system as it speaks.

"Hello, Luna, is it?" I respond to the voice and watch as a lovely woman emerges from a tree.

"You are a highly smart youngster. Most are unsure of both their location and who I am. She speaks, but I can no longer hear her voice everywhere.

I must admit that I didn't anticipate seeing you working in a grassy field. You appear to be more of a businesswoman. Taking in the moon goddess, I say. Although several people claim she was wearing a dress when she spoke to them, she is quite attractive and is not. Her feet are naked, and she is dressed in pants and a OneRepublic shirt that she has removed the sleeves from.

"Most individuals enjoy the field. Although they claim it is soothing, I didn't make you like most people. She says, and in an instant, we're in a board room that looks a lot like the one where all the Oregon pack trainers gather. "Better?"

"Much. What do we need to talk about next? Now that I'm comfortable, I ask.

"I need you to visit your grandfather's house tomorrow and request to see the newborn's birth certificate and all the infant pictures. When you witness it, you will comprehend. After that, speak with your father so that you can determine what to do. She claims. To continue, I nod and turn to face her. I had forgotten how tolerant you are. People usually hate it when I'm so mysterious.

Well, you can't just tell folks what will happen in the future. That advantage would be abused, or others would take action to try to change it. People's ignorance of the fact that their actions are the only thing securing the future is amusing. Rolling my eyes, I say.

"Right! You understand! I ought to invite you around more frequently. As she speaks, she reclines in her chair and places her feet on the desk. I ought to invite you around more frequently. OH! What a reminder. There will be a change, and it will be stressful. There will be a conflict, but it will be for the best. I won't say too much. She says while appearing irritated.

She smiles at me as I nod and then gives me one last notion. Don't be frightened to adore him, is all I think before I start to fade.

~

My head is on Axe's lap when I awaken on the couch, and Whiskey is smiling softly at the two of us.

I intended to wake you two up. I was, in fact. I merely wished to savor the tranquility for a while. You two are deserving.

"It's ok. I appreciate you letting him rest. With a war going on, there won't be much time for sleep. I wish I had more to say. I say as I approach him. Before heading upstairs, I give him a hug and kiss on the cheek as I bid him goodbye. I lay down, only vaguely understanding what tomorrow may bring.

The next morning, I get up and go about my routine before taking a shower, getting dressed, and eating breakfast. The plans for the day were discussed with everyone present at the dinner table. As everyone shared their intentions, my mother's suggestion—who hadn't had much time to do so—was to go explore the area.

"I figured we could go through your old baby photos together, I guess. I want to see some of yours, and you brought some of mine. You've been telling me for a while that you need to get a hold of your birth certificate, too. I tell my mother, who gives me a horrified expression.

"MANY THANKS! I keep forgetting that I wanted to inquire about that. My mother claims—and I am confident—that she will accept the schedule change.

"You don't have a copy of your birth certificate?" Cassandra inquires while cocking her head to gaze at my mother.

"No, I didn't have time to grab anything when my mother disowned me since she constantly guarded critical documents. I got a job thanks to whiskey without any of that. She clarifies.

"He did a really lovely thing. Without a doubt, go grab that. and images of infants? Do you happen to have some Cassie on you? She must have been a cute young child. Cassandra says while grinning and turning to face me.

"I did. We can examine them prior to dinner. And she was the sweetest baby!" Mom says while wearing a broad smile. I'm content as long as she is, too.

That is nice to hear. I'll also pull out the baby pictures of my kids. According to Cassandra, she and my mother plan over breakfast.

I hop in the car with my mum and the beta and Axe after breakfast today. We don't have much time to contemplate during the short travel, which leaves me with little opportunity to plan. I detest traveling without a plan, so this trip has confused me. I sincerely hope everything works out after this.

We all exit the vehicle and enter the home together. As his sister's feet are leaving the ground, Andrew rushes down the steps and grabs her in a bear grip. Before he puts her back on the ground, he swirls her around while she giggles.

You saw me yesterday, Andrew. You don't have to do this daily!" She chuckled.

"I need to make up for missing you for 18 years. Thus, I must perform this action each day. He states forcefully before turning to face me as grandfather Marcus gives mom a hug. Hey, youngster! How are you doing?

"I've done well. Could we view some of Mom's old baby pictures and other items, such as her birth certificate? When I inquire, the two of them exchange glances.

That shouldn't pose a challenge. If Stella didn't bring them along—which I don't know why she would—that is. This time, Grandpa says as he makes his way back up the stairs.

"I'm puzzled as to why she would. I haven't actually ever seen my birth certificate, though, as I just realized. It wasn't necessary for my job in the pack, so I didn't have to worry about it, and I didn't just think about it at random. Says Andrew. Grandpa returns down with a box of items that seemed quite light around ten minutes later.

All I could discover was this. Since I saw Andy's birth certificate, I believe yours is also present. She had great organization. He says as he places the box on the coffee table's top.

Andrews' papers are on top, just as he stated. everything, including his auto insurance details and medical records. The following section includes a good number of images from mom and Andy's youth. We look through the birthday images, and it becomes clear that I am a perfect replica of my young mother. There can't be more than 150 images of the two of them between when we start looking at them and when we reach the bottom of the box. The fascinating part comes when we get to Mom's records. She has very no information about herself as an infant, very few medical records, and school records. Her birth certificate, though, is by far the most intriguing document.

Although her last name is different, it contains her name. Not Mora, at all. This is Lustan. Marcus is not identified as her father either. Marcus was looking down at the paper in pain while looking at me, Mom, and Andrew in perplexity.

"Daddy? Lucas Lustan, who is he? Mom queries, pointing to the name listed under "Father."

I wasn't a true mate for your mother. Forced matings were commonplace in the past. Typically, they were power plays. Your mother and I were among the few of them that existed. Most people were really hesitant to tamper with Luna's plan, but her father and I weren't concerned about it. She and I had never been fans of the notion, but after the death of my partner, I had come to accept it. I am aware that she never did, which is why she departed. We were relieved of our duty after the recent passing of her father. I admire her for sticking around for so long. We dated when she was 19 and I was about to turn 21, and we got married when I was 18 and she was 17. When she was 18 years old, she came upon a rouge while running in the woods.

Her mate is Lucas Lustan. He takes a moment to catch his breath and then resumes.

Before her father learned about it and had him killed, she had been seeing him in secret for a year. After that, we were compelled to mate. I learned that we were expecting you a week and a half later. I was overjoyed to be having a child. Our fathers were upset when we learned you were a girl and told us we would have to carry on until we produced a boy. Ari, you still hadn't even been born. It was crazy. But we had to do what we were told. Now that I think about it, I see that you didn't arrive early. Since you weren't mine, you were exactly on time. His voice breaks as he finishes the sentence.

My mother sprang to her feet and ran to embrace my father as he started crying. I'm sure my mother was crying as well, and Andrew swiftly joined the group of grieving people.

Oh, daddy, I'm yours forever. You were the one who reared me and gave me an unwavering affection. You will forever be my father. Through her tears, she speaks. Due to the intense emotions in the room, I can feel my inner wolf prowling, and I immediately think of my mother.

My wolf is anxious by the emotions in the room, so I'm going for a walk. "Ok honey, just be back in an hour and take one of the males with you. If you need me, call me."

I nod to Axe and motion for him to follow me after that final thought. He exhales deeply as we move outside.

"I'm grateful. There, the air was incredibly dense. Before speaking to me, he takes a second deep breath and gives me a worried WA look. Are you alright?

"Yeah just worried. Come for a stroll with me? I make a head gesture and enquire.

"I'm interested. Any specific location? With his hands in his pockets, he asked while striding alongside me.

"I've got a place in mind." We then set out for my father's workplace. The trip to his office is quick, and at this point the beta is aware to just pass me through with a mind link to Cole. When we stand up to knock on the office door, someone calls us in.

Hey, kid. He sees me and asks, "How are you doing? He signals for Axe to take a seat where I've already taken one and nods to me.

"I have important news that needs to be shared immediately." He nods in agreement, allowing me to continue. We were mistaken about my mother's name.

He raises one eyebrow into his hairline and asks, "What?"

Ari Mora is not my mother's legal name. Ari Lustan is here. I slowly speak.

"How did you learn about this?" He asks with a dubious tone.

Her birth certificate was being examined. It was revealed that Lucas is her biological father and not Marcus. I try to explain, but it's clear that he is still skeptical of the circumstances.

"How do you know it's real?"

The Luna told me something significant was about to occur yesterday night. I say.

The question "What does that mean for me?"

"If you used Mora to reject Mom, then you might not have rejected Mom in Luna's eyes."

"However, she accepted the denial. She was suffering as a result of it. He asks with a confused and hurt expression on his face. He was never pardoned for that by his wolf.

Look, think about it in prayer, and I'll advise mum to follow suit. Without a good reason, Luna wouldn't have mentioned her birth certificate. I remark while getting up and approaching Axe. "I won't force you two to accept one another, but if my idea is correct, then you two might want to discuss it. Just an idea. Axe is following closely behind me as I walk toward the entrance. As we leave, Cole doesn't say anything, but I can see he's thinking. We bid the beta farewell and still have about 30 minutes to go on our walk, so I advise stopping at a small ice cream parlor.

"Do you really believe that such a small detail caused the rejection to fail?" While we are eating our ice cream and heading towards the house, Axe asks.

"I believe Luna would take such action to ensure the success of her plan for her children. I believe that even a seemingly insignificant information could have a big impact in the future. And I really hope they manage to resolve it. I believe that my mother's want to be around him is the result of the wrong kind of rejection. In addition, I am aware that Cole misses her and would quickly retract his denial. They deserve a genuine opportunity at this, and in my opinion, this is it. I share with him my sincere wishes and opinions.

He says, as if it weren't the most apparent thing in the world, "You care deeply about your mother."

"Sure, that. I am aware that at some point I must leave the nest, yet for the longest time I was all that she had. I simply can't bear the idea of leaving her. Even though her father and brother are not blood relatives, she is happy to have them back in her life. I still want her to be close by so she can visit her seven grandchildren and more easily become a part of their lives. I say in reference to the joke we told previously. "I want her to be happy above all else and to be there for me if I need help. She made such a great sacrifice for me; now it's my time.

"That is entirely reasonable. I'm delighted you told me about that. We finish our ice cream, he continues, and then we get to Marcus and Andrew's house. We enter a home where there is much joy and laughing. It's a welcome diversion from the previous weeping. When we enter the living room, they are laughing and looking at the baby pictures. I join them at the coffee table and can't help but laugh. The remainder of the time is spent laughing.

Alpha's Daughter Rejected: Chapter 15

Cole's POV

I'm not sure how to react to the information that was given to me. Due to a technicality, I got a second opportunity with my companion. When I told Cassie that I wanted a real shot to be a family, I wasn't lying. I wish I could meet and hug her mother. I want to have children someday. Because of my partying tendencies, which I deeply regret, I missed a lot of things. I'm hoping Cassie is right and her mother will accept my apology. Although I am aware that the confidence won't be immediately restored, I would appreciate a chance.

'Please, Luna, give me wisdom and courage. I want a real opportunity to make up for my error and become the guy you want me to be. I am aware that I don't deserve it, yet you have shown yourself to be a goddess of mercy. I merely hope that I can win your approval. I promptly say a prayer and get back to the task at hand.

Hello, bossman. I have a question, please. Walking in and sitting down, according to my beta.

"Was not that a question just then?" I make a mocking retort.

I said, "Ha ha ha." Before moving on, he says, rolling his eyes. that is the girl that keeps appearing and disappearing?

I sigh and take a time to consider my answer. Until I give you permission, I trust you not to tell... Cassie Mora is who she is. She is my child.

The question "You have a daughter?" He asks, his eyes wide.

"Yes. Her mother is my mate, and 18 years ago, when I was high on power, I 'rejected' her. Ari Mora is her mother. Ari is giving me the opportunity to get to know my daughter while they are visiting her brother and father.

"Why did you put quotes around 'rejected'?"

"That's something else. Her birth certificate was examined, and they discovered that she is not actually Marcus' daughter. Her last name isn't Mora in formal documents, so my rejection might not have been sincere.

"Boss, that's pretty serious stuff. If the rejection wasn't valid, what would you do?

That is my current predicament. I'm looking forward to the goddess's tranquility. I fear that the rejection did hold and that I will never have a chance to start a family because of a careless error I made, yet I want the rejection to have failed so much that I can have a chance at doing so. I explain while leaning back on the chair.

I'll let you know what. Why don't you go rest as the Luna is rumored to appear in dreams. I'll let the pack know that you're not feeling well right now, but you can attempt to gather your thoughts. When you're mentally exhausted and stressed out, you can't anticipate peace. He says as he approaches the desk while standing.

"Man, that sounds good. I'll accept your offer. I straighten up and give him a big brother hug before heading into my room. I get into bed, covering myself completely, and closing my eyes. I fall asleep immediately after waking up.

I'm on a hill covered in flowers when I wake up, and I realize I'm dreaming. All at once, I hear voices coming from everywhere and nowhere.

"Child." The voice from above says. "I have heard your prayers, and I have come to answer them."

I quickly get down on my knees and bow. It's a pleasure to be in your company, Luna. I only ask for your advice.

"My child, I brought you into the world for my instruction. I'm here to break the bad news to you because I've seen your heart and how your character has grown. You've developed, and I've given you a chance to restore your happiness. Ari is the only thing holding you back. If my plan is to work, you two will need to act and think like the adults I know you are. I haven't had a chance to speak with her yet, but you two need to meet at your convenience and chat like the adults I know you are.

"Sure, that. Luna, I'll try to abide by your requests. Never having raised my head, I say.

"I really do, kid. I'm now awake.

I abruptly get out of bed and notice that it is already beyond four o'clock as I turn to look at my clock. I truly hope we can resolve this.

From Ari's perspective

After reading the story and crying for at least 15 minutes, we spent the rest of the afternoon looking over the photos that had been taken up until my 17th birthday. Stella then claimed that we were too old and no longer required photographs. She never showed me love, but she was also never excessively accommodating. She didn't like me, and I could feel it, but I never found out why. Even after hearing the tale, I still don't understand why she detested me. You'd think she'd want to hang onto the last piece of her mate she had.

The trip back to Axe's pack wasn't as quiet as I had anticipated. The universe must have slowed down as a result of the events that occurred since the chat lasted for hours and I was left with a terrible headache.

"Mom. I have a hypothesis.

"And what exactly is that theory, my love?"

That the mate link has been having an impact on you even if it was never truly broken. I have a time to digest what she says.

"Elaborate." I say, a hint of authority in my voice. I detest having to use it, but right now it appears that I have somewhat lost control over my wolf. She didn't appear to be bothered by my tone, even though I was still upset with myself for using it on my kid.

"I believe that the mate tie was never fully severed because he didn't use your legal last name. that it still exists and that's why you're still experiencing its consequences. The Luna released you from the bond but did not actually break it when you accepted his rejection. She pauses to exhale fully. I think you and Cole could rekindle their connection if you wanted to.

I remained silent and buried myself in meditation after that. That is what gave the impression that the vehicle ride took an eternity. My mind decided to wander, which is never a good thing. I couldn't help but feel as though we might be able to have a true family. to help raise our grandchildren and watch our daughter mature and find her true love. to age together, however slowly that may be. Was there a chance for us to be happy?

These were the ideas that sent me to sleep, and the dream that followed was one I hadn't had in almost 18 years. I realized I was in the world of the goddess when I woke up in a lush field with the glorious sky above me.

"You worry too much, kid. I've given you a plan, and it was on the verge of failure once. Don't let it occur once again. I used a little technicality to give you a second opportunity. You two need to make an effort to make it work if I want you two together. He's finally developed into the man I envisioned for him. Accept him and help him develop. Luna said, never once appearing in my line of sight. She gave a brief lecture before returning me to my bed. I was so worn out from the previous day that my quick awakening was short-lived, and before I had a chance to process what the Luna had said, I had fallen back to sleep for some proper rest.

Alpha's Daughter Rejected: Chapter 16

Cassie's POV

This morning as I woke up, I was going to begin my usual routine when my mother interrupted me. Although she enjoys working out, she won't get up this early, so I know something isn't quite right.

My mother mumbles, "Baby," so as not to wake up our hosts. Is your father aware of your theory?

"Yes. I told him as I was walking. It felt proper at that time to give him an opportunity to consider it as well.

"Ok. I believe you. You have never done anything to even threaten to erode my trust, much less do so. You should be present because I need to speak with your father.

But I have training today, as much as I would love to. We're still figuring out a schedule, but I could probably-" she interrupts me, which is something she never does.

"No, it's fine, I just need to go talk to your father about something, but I won't ask you to miss it because I know you'll be busy and have other commitments. I am able to speak to your father on my own. Most likely, that would be better.

Mom, are you certain? I'm not afraid to request a day off since I can take it.

I'm confident I can handle that man, baby. I want to know if he will be responsive since you've lately spoken to him.

"Yes. He's previously admitted to me that he would return his rejection in a heartbeat if given the chance. He despises himself and wishes he could alter himself because of what he has done for you. He was more than open to the concept.

At least I now have assurance that it won't fail. You remain here and take care of your business, and I'll discuss everything with your father while you stay here. I really hope this works." I want us to live as a unit.

"Mom, I know. If doing this will make you happy, then that is what I want because I want you to be happy.

You're going to find your soul mate soon, baby. You ought to be more concerned about your happiness than mine. Furthermore, if your father and I reconcile, we'll have to move, and before long, you'll be old enough to decide where you live. My love, you must put yourself first.

"Mom, when the time is right, we'll worry about that. I'll get ready for training while you go get ready to meet Cole. Tell me how it turns out. I advise giving her a head-kissed kiss. She enters her room after walking over to it, while I leave to go for a run. I return just in time for breakfast as mom is outlining her agenda for the day, but she just grabs an apple rather than joining them for breakfast. Before doing a lot of exercise, I don't want to overeat and end up feeling ill.

And such was the course of my day. I admit that I didn't eat much, which was bad, and I spent the majority of the day training. I could hardly move when I was finally finished with my workout. I took a shower and headed to my room to file the report we were required to write when I noticed I was missing all of the necessary files. I reluctantly get up and head over to Axe's office to pick up the paperwork.

I knock on his door when I arrive at his office and only get a faint "come in." I enter and start to speak, but he glances up and leans back in his chair while patting his lap. I carefully approach him, sit in his lap, and rest against his chest. As soon as he kisses my forehead, my wolf begins to purr. The question "What's wrong, love?" I'm on the verge of nodding off when he asks in a soothing tone.

"I'm sore because I don't think you understand how fast these kids learn so I've had to boost them again today and oh my gosh that feels nice," the person said. "I'm weary and still have paperwork to do. I have to eat so I don't pass out. As my amazing partner begins to massage my shoulders, I pause to say something.

Why don't you sit in this room and do the papers while I have Grandpa bring us some food and provide an explanation? He claims to be giving me random head kisses.

"Hmm, a break, food, and time with the most wonderful man in the world? Sounds fantastic. I suggest giving him a nose kiss.

"Mmm. May I?" As he speaks, he turns to face me.

"If you didn't, I'd be disappointed." I meet him halfway and give him a soft kiss, which makes my stomach fluff up. He passes me the files I originally came in for as I climb off his lap and seat in the chair I had brought up to the desk across from him. Whiskey brings in two plates of food, and until forks start clattering against plates, we sit calmly and work.

We immediately finished our job and cuddled for approximately an hour after Whiskey removed our plates after we finished eating. We decided it would be best to sleep in our individual rooms as we were drifting off to sleep. Thanks to the Luna's design, we won't have to do that for too much longer, which is good because we sleep better cuddled up together.

The moment my mother entered the room and sat down on my bed, I hesitantly made my way back to the one I had been given. She gave a soft sigh, and I sat down next to her so we could discuss how it went.

"How much has he changed. It's obvious that the connection was never truly severed. I sense how strongly my wolf and his wolf are tugging toward one another, and I sense a really powerful thing pulling us together. She begins to ramble but quickly stops.

"Any other things?" I inquire because I am aware that she is silent.

Being apart from him right now aches. I'm not sure just how long I can avoid him. I would accompany you to take you back to Risen Moon and everything, but I know that I'll soon have to tell Liam and Lilly that I'm transferring here.

"Mom, I'm moving if you are. In addition, I'm having a hard time leaving here for something.

Oh, will you let me know? She asks, standing up and angling her body toward me.

In due course. You currently have a concern, and I'll let everyone know when it's more resolved. I speak, and I'm confident she hears me.

"Well, I'm happy. Whatever it is, I hope it makes you happy. My forehead is kissed by her.

"Trust me, mom, it does." As she exits the building and heads for her room, I say with a smile.

With a smile on my face and tiredness ingrained in my bones, I eventually laid down for the night. The day was enjoyable. They are always the ones when you can hardly move after exercising.

Alpha's Daughter Rejected: Chapter 17

Ari's POV

Although I was a little more anxious than I would have been if Cassie had been present, I was still confident in my ability to manage the situation. There was only Cole. He has changed, yes, but it has changed for the better, so why am I concerned? Why am I nervous now when I'm never nervous? Okay, so maybe I do feel a bit worried, and perhaps when I do, I tend to ramble, but rambling is a common trait among people, and being nervous is nothing new. Ari, pay attention now!

I take a deep breath and cut off my internal dialogue before it can continue. I walk with my head held high to my friend's office, prepared to take on the world. or at least in this circumstance. When I arrive at his office, the beta waves me through to his workspace. I rap on the door once I arrive. He only needs to shout for a brief while for me to enter. We examine each other as I enter the room and take a deep breath. It's fortunate that I took that deep breath since all it took was one look to steal my breath.

She was correct. The relationship was never entirely severed. While struggling to catch his breath again, he speaks.

Yes, she is a good person. The finest thing to ever happen to me was meeting her. Without her, I'm not sure who or what I would be. So I thank you on her behalf. I nod and express my gratitude to him.

Come sit down. He points to the chair across from him and says. I do, and we both sit still for a while. Why are we acting so awkwardly, ugh? Even a simple chat is impossible between us even though we should be in love.

Yes, it seems as though we are strangers or something.I say, my voice dripping with sarcasm.

"All right, the sass is unnecessary." He averts his gaze.

However, we are in fact strangers. The only things we know about one another are what we just found out and that we have a kid in common. Although I can see your assumption that we would be madly in love and all that jazz, that's not how things operate.

"I know. How is she doing? I mean our daughter.

She had teaching experience, or else she wouldn't be here. I had to argue with her to acquire that one, but playing the mom card together with a dash of notoriety will persuade her to pay attention. What I'm trying to express is that she tried to cancel her training. "That makes sense. I love her, but she can be a pain. She's amazing because of how you reared her.

"I wasn't really active. She was so self-reliant that despite my best efforts to raise her, she essentially raised herself. She would walk around as if they weren't there even though I would have others to monitor her while I worked a lot. At the age of 3, if I wasn't home, she prepared meals for herself. She was a determined person who would pursue her goals no matter what.

"At three, she was cooking for herself? 3 years old, exactly? If she had help, why would she do that?

She never sought assistance. She would discard them as if they were flies when they tried to assist. I will give her credit for trying to be courteous about it.

"So she's always been on her own?"

"Very. I had a fantastic baby because to the Luna up top. She was extremely intelligent and hardly ever cried. The only negative, in my opinion, was that she conversed with strangers, but that was always advantageous. Better child could not have been desired. As I consider my Cassie, I can't help but smile.

"I'm pleased you kept that information from me. You needed her more than I did, and I had a lot of maturing to do. We both would have suffered since I wouldn't have been able to care for her as much as she deserved. More than I needed her, you did. The Luna is skilled at what she does.

"Yeah, I'm not sorry I didn't tell you. In all honesty, I still need her. I needed her.

"I am at odds. I don't believe you require her. I believe you attempt to cling to her because you did for such a long time. One day, I hope you'll hang on to me, but for now, I'll make do with holding on to you. As he crouches in front of me and cups my jaw, he speaks.

What will happen once you leave? My eyes start to water at the prospect, so I have to ask.

"I won't abandon you once more. Since I've only recently reconnected with you, the past 18 years without you have been like living in hell. I never had the chance to truly love you, and I won't let that opportunity pass me by now. Although I may not know you as well as I should, I do want to. I'm so close to loving you right now, though. I'm hoping that one day you'll love me. because I'll be there to catch you this time. He says, and I can sense admiration in his eyes.

That's just the bond speaking, I said. I can't help but feel unconfident. Everyone in my life rejected me, with the exception of my daughter and pack. That is a lot of time for negative self-talk.

"No. No, it's not, I promise. The purpose of the link is merely to demonstrate to us what we are unable to see on our own. Booping me on the nose, he says.

I look into his eyes and cannot detect any hint of lying. I gave it some more thought before making a statement that could never be retracted because I am aware that the bond isn't intended to compel us to be together.

"If you're willing, I'm willing too." I can't help but give him my own wet smile in response to his brilliant smile.

"If you're willing, I'm willing too. I'm more than ready. He continues, "And I kiss my soulmate for the first time in 18 years."

Alpha's Daughter Rejected: Chapter 18

Axe's POV

To be able to hold my partner in public makes me happy. Don't get me wrong, I adore our private times together, but I would prefer to always have her in my arms rather than just in my office. I'm prepared to introduce Luna to the pack and see her step into the part. I'm more than ready for her to talk the talk because she already walks the walk. I'm prepared to establish a family and a life. Without having to worry about stupid teens hitting on her, I'm ready to hold her at night in our own bed. I wish I could tell her that she is mine. Even though I doubt she would wear a dress, I want to witness her go down the aisle.

Would Grandpa Whiskey be able to assist me in finding a ring? I don't want my parents or siblings to know anything. Will she want me to request her father's consent? Would she want him to accompany her on her wedding day? Would she even want a lavish wedding or would she prefer to simply go to court? Even though we haven't had a formal date yet, I've already started to consider getting married. Would she be interested in that? I'm aware that I'm already in love, and that my feelings for the women I'm connected to have nothing to do with the relationship. I could not have asked for a greater companion. Every day I give thanks to The Luna above for providing me with the best. I don't know what I done to deserve her. Whiskey drops a huge on my desk, startling me out of my reverie.

"Finally! You've been gone for approximately twenty minutes, boy! Focus! Your lads are attempting to communicate with you, and I also have some news for you. In essence, Whisk shouts in my ear.

"Are you considering your buddy boss? Do you still see her eyes when it is dark? James, my beta, queries. Whiskey asks, "Do they know?" as it turns to face me.

"Yeah. When all you can see is her eyes, you might infer why it's difficult to concentrate.

Yes, I can envision that.

"So, what exactly are we talking about?"

Just providing you with the most recent reports. With the exception of some border guides fighting, nothing very exciting. While they were in that state, a few rogues attempted to assault, which startled them. The rouges were short-lived. Rylie, my gamma, said.

When did that take place? Not remembering, I enquire.

2 hours ago. We only recently learned about it—maybe 20 minutes ago. Rylie says, shrugging.

"Alright. Does anything else? They respond "no" and go on when I ask. Okay, Whiskey, what's going on?

"We'll soon have to inform them. Nearly one month has passed since you informed them of it.

They will discover soon enough. Her business shouldn't take too long, in my opinion.

"And what if it does?"

That's something I need to discuss with her. Is that the topic you came to discuss?

"No. They are asking every Alpha and their mate to attend the ball in two weeks and the business meeting we have next month. Present and past. We will all be present. By then, I had hoped to have a new Alpha Female and perhaps an heir.

Grandpa, we have to wait till after our marriage and even then, we have to wait until she is 18 years old.

"So, have children been brought up?"

Yes, there had recently been a conversation.

"And how many do you plan?"

"Seven." I mention the joke she told earlier. We wouldn't be able to manage seven kids, in my opinion.

Good luck with that, I suppose. Hopefully you're kidding. You two are going one for two, I see. Do you prefer any certain genders?

"Healthy. I don't care what gender it is; I simply want to be healthy. Although I will always love them.

You have always been a bright child. I can comprehend. There was a knock on the door while Whiskey was speaking, and he smiled slightly.

"Entro." I address the person at the door. The moistest, most gorgeous woman I've ever seen enters as soon as it opens.

"Hello, Cassie."

Welcome, Whiskey. Have I been rude? She inquires while examining both of us.

"Never! I was about to go talk to the cooks about dinner as I was about to leave. Now I have to go do it. After saying this, Whiskey stepped out the door and shut it behind him.

"What's up, Sweet Pea?" She slouches in the seat next to me and I inquire. I have never seen her in a more casual setting than this.

"I'm really worn out. The good news is that we won't have to keep our identity a secret for very long. Everything is coming together, and we can be exposed as soon as it falls. From her slouched position, she speaks. I get up and walk over to her, leaning over and asking if I can kiss her. I can't control the silly smile that spreads across my face. I smother her face in small kisses when she responds "yes."

"I'm very happy. What date do you anticipate?

"I need to get all the details in order before I can give you a date, but I'm hoping less than a week."

"Awww, I was really hoping for one."I quip while pouting jokingly.

"Soon, Love." She asks if she can kiss me and adds with a smile. Yes, of course, I reply, and we kiss before being forced to part ways.

Do you need anything in particular? Or did you simply arrive carrying good news? I inquire as I sit down again.

"I merely came to join you in celebrating this happy event. I have to go back to my room and get dinner ready.

Of course, My Love, I want to wish you a wonderful night. At the evening dinner, I'll see you.

I will desire to see your face until then. With the sweetest smile, she said.

Alpha's Daughter Rejected: Chapter 19

Cassie's POV

I'm so relieved that everything is now going according to plan. Though I'm not sure if I'll be able to call him dad just yet, I can't wait to see my mom content with her partner. Living somewhere other than Oregon has been strange, and it still doesn't seem like home. Despite the fact that my partner is here, I have spent my entire life in a different setting, therefore it will take some time for me to get used to the new location. Although it's fairly lovely and not overly heated thanks to my wolf genes, I haven't explored enough of the area yet. I heard there are a lot of deer, so that will be nice for hunting, but aside from that, I erred by failing to conduct enough environmental study.

I'm currently training some of the adolescent pack members at Axe's pack while Mom and Cole are out on a covert date so they can't yet tell the packs about their mating. I'm quite proud of them because they've learnt how to act around me and because they take their training seriously. Bullying, which I have made it very clear I would not accept, has not come to my attention. Someone almost started to bully me, but I raised my eyebrow and stopped them. I'm eager to learn more about my mother's date now that training is almost complete.

A few kids stay behind to assist me clean up the practice field after I release the teens for the day, and the majority head to the shower. When we're done, I take a shower before starting my day's paperwork, which is perhaps the most difficult aspect of the job. Since I had to complete the paperwork back home, I'm fairly accustomed to it, but it doesn't make it any simpler. I want to eat and take a nap so badly, but I have to stay awake. I need to stop taking so many naps now before I mess up my sleep schedule.

I get the paperwork I need to complete for the training and sit down in my room to start working on it. My mother enters the room while I'm still working and leaps into my bed. She always smiles, which makes it strange for me because she never did when I was a child.

Hello, mom? That well? I smile down at her and inquire.

"Yes. I'm overjoyed. He's going to present me to the pack as their Female Alpha in two days after we started planning the Mate Ceremony. The ceremony will take place in three days, followed by the Alpha Female ceremony two days later since we don't want to make you wait too long.

"So, when is the human wedding?" I request a change to my reading classes.

"We haven't yet talked about it. The majority of the details for the other three things were completed today, but we'll have to talk about that tomorrow.

"Good sounds. Tomorrow I'm meeting with Axe, so you should definitely phone Liam and Lilly and ask them to get our stuff ready. We won't be able to go fetch it outside, in my opinion. You are aware of how much companions detest being apart. He probably won't be able to take off long enough from his work as Alpha to accompany us while we pack things.

We get a honeymoon, so he might be able to. I believe he would enjoy visiting Oregon, but again, we'll have to talk about that tomorrow.

"Good sounds. Would you like to hang out in the living room with the ladies while I finish the last of the paperwork?

"That sounds excellent, I agree. I need to change first because I smell like fish.

I'll see you there, I promise. I must first deliver this to Axe, so I'll meet you down there.

I gather the paperwork and enter his office without having to change out of my tank top and spanx. Both of them are quite modest, so I wasn't concerned. His office door opened immediately when I rapped on it.

He is sitting at his desk with his own pair of reading glasses on as I walk in, and he gives me a fleeting glance before glancing back down. When he realizes it's me, he then does a double take.

Hello, sweetheart. How are you doing? He asks, stopping all he is doing.

"Good. I was only here to deliver the day's documents. and let you know that we are able to divulge our relationship to you.

"Really?" He asks, his eyes filled to the brim with optimism.

"Yep. In two days, my parents will make the announcement that she is the Alpha Female, followed by their mate ceremony in three days, then the Alpha ceremony a few days later. With your permission, I would like to tell my mom today because I don't want to steal the spotlight from her when she's having a huge moment, but I also don't want to wait. Her response will help me plan more effectively.

"That's more than fair, in my opinion. I merely want you to smile.

"All I want is you. I'd rather not wait any longer. My inability to be with you is killing me. And I detest hiding things. He enfolds me in his arms while I speak.

"I always get you. If it means that your mother will be content, I can wait a little longer. She plays a significant role in your life, therefore I don't want you to feel as though you must keep our connection a secret or go public because of me. I'll be ready for you at all times.

I appreciate you for that. We can let your family and team know tomorrow if you wish. I'll let my mom know first thing in the morning, and then we can all meet up for lunch. Really, I don't care.

"I think that notion is fantastic. But not as much as I love you," he adds, giving my nose the tiniest kiss. I put one on his and untie myself from him so I can visit my mum below. I am incredibly fortunate to have found this man to be my life mate.

Alpha's Daughter Rejected: Chapter 20

Cassie's POV

After dinner, my mother and I returned to my room and sat on my bed. I was unsure of how my upcoming action would affect my mother's unwavering grin.

"Momma?" Unsure of how to approach the topic, I inquire in a soft voice.

Do you mean "yes, baby girl?"

"I have something I want to tell you."

"You know you can tell me anything, little girl," I said.

"I met my travel companion early on. I didn't tell you because I wanted you to pay attention to your dad, brother, and then Cole. I feel more prepared to openly accept him now that everything has been resolved and you are arranging your rituals.

"So, baby, who is it?"

Beta Axe. We verbally acknowledged our link in front of The Luna, but we kept it quiet because initially, I wanted to be able to concentrate only on him. However, I no longer feel the need to keep it a secret from anyone. I don't want to steal your thunder, but I love him and I don't want to keep it a secret.

"Tell the world, my love. Do not conceal your partner. Although I can see your motivation, you shouldn't. If anyone tries to steal my thunder, Cole's pack will have it. In this pack, you will rule the roost. Be content. She brushes a strand of my hair out of my face and whispers, "Live your life," with the kindest grin I've ever seen on my mother. Go see him. It must be difficult for the two of you that he is so close but still so far away. You two sleeping in the same room is fine in my book. so long as it is only dozing. I'm not ready to become a grandmother yet.

Certainly, mum. I stand up, give her a head kiss, and then go into the bathroom to put on my pajamas. I finish and proceed down the hall, stopping in front of his door. I lift my hand hesitantly and rap on his door.

"Come on in." My friend's drowsy voice muttered. I walked in after opening the door and was nearly overcome by his incredible aroma. He must have detected my aroma since he shouted my name while looking up in a very sleepy manner. "Cassie? What's going on, baby?

"My mother received the news well. She was also worried that our separation was hurting us or preventing us from getting enough rest. She insisted that we share a room to sleep. I mean sleep strictly. She isn't ready to become a grandmother yet. I say from the foot of his four-poster bed while grinning.

"So why are you still over there, far away?" Come here, I need a hug and am exhausted. As he turns over and raises the covers on the opposite side of the bed, he says. He drew me into his arms after I approached and settled down among the blankets. I sighed contently as I tucked my head into the crook of his neck. I was able to drift off into a long, sound slumber pretty quickly.

The following morning, when we awakened, we couldn't help but relax in each other's arms. When we eventually got up, I went to my room to get dressed and since it wasn't my day to train, I made the unusual decision to put on a dress to surprise everyone. But I can't possibly wear shoes if I'm going to wear a dress.

Because it's so hot outside, the dress I choose has a red plaid skirt and no sleeves. I put on my favorite ring, which my uncle had purchased for my mother when they were younger, together with an anklet I had recently purchased before leaving Oregon. I walk downstairs with my hair pulled back in a ponytail. As I reach the foot of the steps, I look up to see Axe chatting to his mother and grinning.

He's got on a blouse that resembles my dress, some plain pants, and no shoes. Unintentionally, we have matched. His wet, unstyled hair is plainly clean but not neat. Can I just mention that my friend has some lovely forearms given that his sleeves are rolled up? He has an Alpha-related marking on his forearm, which is visible when his sleeves are rolled up. Definitely really hot.

"Well, you two look so cute! Have you planned this? His mother glances at the two of us and asks. She might be wary of us now, but we have plans to tell her in a few minutes, so I'm not too concerned.

Hey, mum, how about we have breakfast today? I have a significant announcement to make. As he leads his mother to the table, he speaks. The majority of the normal crowd has already arrived. Grandpa Whiskey is the only person absent; he is aware of the announcement. Since the first day, some locations have become somewhat designated for each of us to sit. Whiskey enters the room, sits down in his chair, looks at his grandson, then at me, before becoming a little more alert.

"Oh! That's what we're doing right now? So, proceed, son. When he understands what is happening, he says.

"Alright. I need to make a significant announcement. Before pausing to take a big breath, he says. "My mate is Cassie. She wanted to be able to concentrate solely on us even though we have known about them since I returned from my trip following their arrival. She can now that her mum is content. So here she is—your future Alpha girl.

His mother gets up, walks over to where I'm sitting, lifts me up, and gives me a hug. His sister almost squeals before standing and bouncing around. My mother approaches him, perhaps to scare him, while the boys all go to congratulate him.

Did you plan the clothing for this, then? His sister responds with a deep, southern drawl.

"No, that was just convenient." I laugh as I say.

So, when can I anticipate having grandkids? Looking between the two of us, his mother says.

"Not for a while, no. Although we haven't talked about a deadline. I guess The Luna has the most influence. I smile as I say.

Well, I'm happy that you two connected. Before resuming her seat, his sister remarks.

"Alright! Let's eat! With that out of the way. While collecting the dish of bacon, Whiskey says. We all chuckle as we eat a delicious meal with friends and family.

Alpha's Daughter Rejected: Chapter 21

Axe's POV

One of the nicest pleasures in the world is seeing the women I love interact with my family. As my family tries to get to know her better and she accepts the interrogation with grace, I can't help but smile. She is undoubtedly the best thing that has happened to me recently. I am eager to begin our life together.

My thoughts are cut off by a call.

I say goodbye and enter the room next door to hear what the caller has to say. My beta has information of an attack on the western frontier. Cassie gets up to join me as I inform my family about it.

Are you leaving it to your beta or are you going to check?

I'm leaving.

If so, I'll accompany you.

"Ok. Although I don't believe there are many, we must move quickly. Can you move around in that?

Nothing matters. I'll change.

"Then, let's go."

We transform into wolves and sprint towards the west boundary, where four irate rouges are waiting. My beta and a few warriors are now holding them off, but I'm more concerned about the three additional rouges who are being protected by a fifth irate rouge. The remaining three rogues are smaller and seem afraid. It resembles a woman and her two kids almost exactly. The dominant wolf changes and puts on a pair of jeans as it hides behind a tree.

"I want to go see my grandchild." A man spoke. He was older, approximately Whiskey's similar age. I move and stroll behind another tree, putting on a pair of pants.

Before I can tell you anything about your granddaughter, I need some basic facts. Starting with your name would be fantastic. Get your guard dogs away from the others you have trapped while you're at it. I declare with confidence in my voice.

Onri Yemin is my name. For loving his partner, my son was murdered.

"I believe you have the incorrect pack," I say. I'm startled when Cassie speaks a little while later because I didn't notice her posture change. She is dressed in one of my shirts, which ends at her mid-thigh.

"What was the name of your son? And his friends?

I'm Will Yemin. Her name escapes me. She was engaged, so they only met in secret. When they were discovered, they were getting ready to flee. He passed away. She was also expecting. I would like to meet her offspring.

"My mate is correct; you are using the incorrect pack. I'm sorry for the pain you must have had, but this is not the one who killed your kid. However, I might be aware of your granddaughter. How recently was this? Cassie remarks while sporting a dejected expression.

"It happened over 40 years ago. Please, kid, don't apologize if you didn't do it. An apology that is not your responsibility wastes your breath. What can you do for me?

"We can talk in more detail there if you would want to follow us to the main office. Calling off the guard dogs will allow us to transport the others to the hospital.

"Boys. Go ahead. Leave the woman alone. The lads comply with his instructions, and when I give him the go-ahead to enter the area, he looks at me for approval before following us and letting us take the initiative.

When we reach the hospital, the warriors check in the woman and her young while my partner, my beta, and I escort Orni to my office. Cassie sits on the outside of my knee as I walk over to my chair and seat down when we arrive. My beta, James, is waiting in the corner, prepared to strike if necessary.

What are your knowledge about my grandchild? More than he asks, he commands. I think there is no malice, and his speech has no influence. It's only desperation.Someone I know has a very similar tale. I'm really close to a woman who recently learned that her mother was engaged to her father's friend but discovered her true love. When he learned that she was sneaking out to visit her boyfriend, her mother's harsh father killed her. Following that, her marriage to her fiancé was hastily consummated. Her father assumed it was her husband's because she didn't tell him she was pregnant until after they were married. When my friend became 18, she ejected her from the home where she had my friend and one other child, a son. My friend's mother just recently got a divorce and moved out. My acquaintance had received verbal abuse from the women because she resembled their mate. It served as a sobering lesson for her.

After a few period of silence, he replies with a small voice strain.

Please let me meet your pal. If she is the daughter of my son, I will know. The risk is worthwhile.

"I'll have her call her down here." My friend says while sporting a sympathetic expression.

I ask her a few questions that have been mildly nagging me while she mentally links her mother.

"What took you so long?" Why do you need to look for your grandchild after nearly 40 years?

"I wish I had looked earlier, but I'm a rogue. I was, in all honesty, too distraught to care for a modest pack. I came dangerously close to losing control of my 'pack'. I had nowhere to look for my missing grandchild. I wasn't in a state of mind where I could act. My sole remaining source of serenity from her passed away, and I was left broken after already losing my companion.

"Then I hope this is your grandchild for your sake. I can't image Cassie being lost.

It is a fate that is worse than death.

"Cassie, what is happening? We've discussed the fact that you can't use the hazy mind links. Ari remarks as she enters the workplace without first knocking. That, I suppose, was one of the 'vague' directions my lovely companion left for her. I can tell that Onri's eyes are misting up because of the small shaking he exhibits as he rises up and turns to face her. Cassie asked, "Who is this?"

It says, "This is Onri Yemin."

"You resemble him so much. also her. We can all hear him whisper, though.

"Who?" Cassie asks in her own almost-whisper.

"My mate and son. Both of them were taken away from me at different periods. Your grandfather is me.

"How? You claim that I resemble your son, but I am unable to verify it. Before I was born, my biological father was killed.

"My kid was murdered for loving his mate despite the fact that she was engaged. We have extremely good grounds for thinking that-"

I am your natural grandchild. "Do I resemble him at all?"

And he resembled my mate exactly.

"Do you have any objections to a DNA test? I don't have any references, and I've already been burned too many times.

"I perceive. I wouldn't be against it.

"Cassie, please ask your dad to meet me here by texting him. I need my partner by my side.

Your partner? What about your stepdaughter Cassie?

She's my daughter, so no. She was born to me. What would lead you to believe that she wasn't?

She never once referred to you as'my friend'. You certainly have a grasp of what I'm referring to.

"I can, yes. I'm sorry, but Cassie is only being cautious in this way.

"I would also want to keep you safe. And I apologize for not being able to earlier.

After a few minutes of their continued conversation, Cole enters and gives his partner a head kiss. He appears startled when they tell him about the morning's activities, including the fact that Cassie and I are friends. It's fantastic to see him making an effort to be a father even if he recognizes it would be foolish of him to oppose and instead threatens me before returning to his mate.

Everyone departs after setting up the blood test, save for Cassie who just sits on my desk. She's still only wearing my shirt, which I just realized, so I'm going to ask someone to get her some appropriate clothing.

Have I mentioned my partner's beauty? mainly because a goddess. If I had no other information, I could have assumed she was The Luna herself. I couldn't have wished for a better partner than her, and she is unquestionably a gift from The Luna.

What did I do to earn her?

Alpha's Daughter Rejected: Chapter 22

Cassandra's POV

It would be an understatement to say that meeting my great-grandfather was unexpected. I can't say I'm upset about it, but I also can't help but be cautious. Although I didn't sense any lying from him, that doesn't imply there wasn't any. Although my instincts are good, they are not flawless.

I still have a sneaking suspicion about the man even as I sit here and discuss the coronation with my future mother-in-law. My mother had faith in him, and she rarely made a mistake, but the length of his mourning and the fact that he lost his companion have me on edge. A male wolf's ability to become feral after losing his mate. The fact that he hasn't yet is astonishing. I turned my attention back to the conversation going on around me and overheard my future sister-in-law and mother-in-law discussing colors. I had informed them that the only thing I truly cared about was getting to pick the outfit. They instantly concurred and assumed control without further ado. Therefore, I'm sitting here oblivious to what will essentially be my wedding. To be frank, I never imagined getting married.

The books are abruptly closed by Cas and Emily, and we hear and smell the boys walking. They have been working outside on some yard upkeep when they enter, but their partner's perfume mostly masks that. I feel bad for Emily since she can only smell the disgusting stench of sweaty men. As my partner approaches to stand behind me, I give her a sympathetic glance, to which she responds with a grateful smile. He glances at his family and smiles softly as he leans on my shoulders.

I'm annoyed because I'm the only one who gets to smell how bad you all smell. Emily replies as she stands up to leave.

Well, that was simple. What exactly were you two discussing?

"Wedding-related stuff." His mother replies.

Then, give the children a break. How about a date for the two of you? Go hang out because I know neither of you actually care about the specifics of the wedding. They should take some time to get to know one another better.

"I guess you're correct. Then you two may depart, but I promise to ground you, son, whether you are a grown Alpha or not, if you don't take a shower. As she got to her feet and followed her husband up the stairs, his mother replied.

"Well, the women spoke. Come on, you can wait while I take a shower in my room. Snoop all you want; I have nothing to hide because we are friends. He adds as he takes me to his room via the stairs. While I read on my phone while lying on his bed, he grabs his clothing and goes to his en suite to take a shower.

Shortly after entering the restroom, he emerges wearing his sleep pajamas. Because I own the same jeans, I am aware that they are from Walmart. The bat symbol is printed on a pair of black jeans. both easy and cozy. This makes him smile at me with a hint of uncertainty, and I can't help but smile at that. He hops into the bed next to me, settles up, and turns to face me so that we are lying like a cliched pair from a teen novel after I simply wave it off.

"So, let's get to know one another." I nod as he asks. You've had how many boyfriends, exactly?

"None. I was never free to even think about dating, and even if I was, I wasn't interested in anyone until I caught a glimpse of your eyes, at which point I was solely interested in you. How are you doing?

When my mother described what a mate was to me when I was around five, I gave up trying with anyone who wasn't my mate. I knew I was finished when I looked into your eyes. Since then, I haven't really thought about anything besides you and my job.

"This makes me happy." I add while grinning a little.

"I'm happy. I enjoy being around you. He says with a beautiful smile and a laugh.

Okay, that was just tacky.

You adore it.

"I love you, but I'm stuck with this part of you,"

It adds to the charm. You wouldn't exchange it for anything else, I'm positive of it.

How could I? You are faultless and the ideal partner for me. Nothing to swap or alter as a result.

Who is being corny right now?

"It adds to the charm," Standing up and going to the kitchen, I say.

That's my line, I say. He calls out to me. I grab an apple for myself and him, some cheese, and some jerky because, well, why not? I can hear the smile in his voice. When I enter the room again, I discover him on his phone. I approach him from behind and encircle him as the tension on his face becomes clear.

"Okay. Soon, we'll be there. I appreciate you telling me. Yes, I will inform her. We'll talk soon. He then hangs up the phone.

"Cole's pack came under attack. It happened so suddenly, and they don't know why. He still wants us to go, despite the fact that none of us were seriously hurt by his pack. Cole merely has a scratch, although he wouldn't tell how big, and your mother is unharmed. They desire our presence there.

"OK. We can go downstairs after I change into some real clothes.

What is wrong with your attire, I ask?

"I'll be wearing pajamas if you are, too. In addition, I'm sick of wearing these tight-fitting jeans.

"Well, that's fair enough. Okay, I'll inform everyone while you put on your pajamas. We'll get some rest when we get home.

"Given that statement, you need to get some rest."

"Combat me. My day was really long.

"Come on, you fools. There's no question Cole was holding back information from us.

Alpha's Daughter Rejected: Chapter 23

Cassie's POV

I wasn't concerned about the trip to Cole's pack. I believed Cole when he stated no one was wounded, even after I witnessed the devastation left in its wake. I started to become anxious when I noticed my mother pacing and waiting on the doorstep. Mom needed a shoulder, therefore I still wouldn't show it.

What's wrong, Mom?

Cole is in the medical area, and I don't want to worry him further because of the seriousness of the cut on his arm.

He claimed it wasn't all that horrible. Good or bad?

"Just a knock on my head, nothing serious. He needed sutures for the wound he received, but until he saw that his pack was okay, he refused assistance. Sweetie, before he returned, the blood loss nearly caused him to pass out.

"All right, let's go see how he is. I'll follow you back on foot.

"Can you come with us, Axel? Cole wants to talk to you about something, I know that.

"Ari, of course.

We all turn around and observe that the injuries are all rather minor. We find Cole on a gurney with an arm covering his eyes and his shirt off, with a scratch running the length of his arm, when we return to the area where physicians are scurrying about like headless birds. It's being sewn up right now because werewolf healing couldn't get to it quickly enough. Cole is obviously in agony because the stitches must stay in for a day or two and painkillers are ineffective in relieving it.

Ah, Cole! Hello, how are you?

"My love, I'm good. Really. What's up? Headache? You seem chilled. thirsty or hungry? Do you need anything? Cole asks, his worry visible on his face. His concern for my mother despite his obvious disability gains him some further respect.

"Cole, give me your worries. You were the one who prevented significant harm for others while still taking the brunt of the pain. Let me worry about you instead of you worrying about me.

I would endure harsher pain for you. What's up, kids?

"Cole, we're good. Do you understand the nature of the attack?

In their most recent battle with sanity, a couple of rouges banded together and chose to launch an attack. At the time, there were three of them and 80 of us, but one was a little more rational. The leader went after me in an effort to gain control of the pack as the other two turned on and murdered each other. At the last minute, he lost his humanity and died. We set the bodies on fire.

"So, it was a one-time event? Shouldn't we not be concerned about yet another targeted attack? While encircling me in his arms, Axel enquires.

"No. It was three insane outlaws. Should I think otherwise, you'll be the first person I notify. While I converse to this young man, why don't you two lovely ladies go for a stroll and grab something to eat. Your mum hasn't yet had dinner, Cassie.

"Make your young man speak. What would you like to eat, baby? I'll deliver something to you. I query Axel.

"I'll eat everything you're eating. I'm not particular. He kisses my forehead, and my mother and I silently walk to the kitchen. The hush, though, is brief. He is kind to you.Mom and I both respond at once. We both smile and joke at one another.

I appreciate Cole's efforts. He brings you joy and treats you the way you ought to have been treated years ago. I hope your partnership is successful. "Ditto, my love.

We get food and deliver it back to the boys, who are talking about how Axel treats and cares for me right. Cole would probably laugh, but I can't help but smile. I give him the dad speech while cracking a small smile, but I cut him off with food. When food is present, they both become animated. Mom sends us home after we dine in a largely silent atmosphere since she will be spending the night with Cole.

We return to the vehicle and exit the area while still holding hands. We quickly update the group before going up to bed. We wear matching jammies and go to bed next to each other.

Alpha's Daughter Rejected: Chapter 24

Cassie's POV

I couldn't help the happiness I felt as I stood next to my mother, who was getting her makeup done while seated in front of a vanity. My mother was joyful because she was getting married, had a relationship, and would soon be treated like a queen. She appears to be really anxious, but you can still tell that she is joyful. She stands up after getting her hair and makeup done and begins to pace the room, leaving the blue dress she's wearing in a graceful trail. It was strange to see her with her hair up and minimal makeup. My mother has never seemed this frazzled or dressed up.

~~~~~~~~~~~~~~

She is gorgeous beyond belief. If only I could calm her down quickly before she starts to perspire out her makeup.

"Mom. Settle down. You're worrying unnecessarily. This man adores you and would sacrifice everything for you. As I approach her, I say, "Sit down," and I help her onto the couch in the designated space.

"I know. It's just a significant adjustment. We've gone from being just the two of us on our own to traveling further than ever before, and you're growing up so quickly. I simply don't know how to deal with all that is happening so quickly.

"With the poise of a queen and your head held high." I reply, grinning at her. "You told me that while I was growing up. When times were bad, you carried yourself with dignity and royal grace. Be an apple. Be menacing outside and charming inside by standing tall and donning a crown.

"It's not simple. You of all people need to be aware of that.

It's time to mature. You are given another opportunity at love. One that you're ready to accept. Furthermore, I'm not really traveling that far. Even after we have children, you'll be able to come visit frequently and see your grandchildren. But for the time being, concentrate on moving forth and becoming what the Luna above intended for you to be. I say and give her a head kiss.

You're supposed to hear this lecture from me on the day of your wedding, I said. We both laugh as she says this.

"Well, I'll take it later today," she said. Why are you making me wear a dress when I'm getting married? I can't believe it. However, I can understand why you wouldn't wear white to your own wedding. That is not at that surprising.

"I've never been a big proponent of upholding tradition. Additionally, it counts because anything blue is on the list. Her father knocks on the door as she draws in a long breath.

"You appear fantastic. I'm not yet prepared to part with you. I have just returned you. As he approaches his daughter, he says while wiping away tears from his eyes. Before also approaching my mother, my uncle waits in the doorway for the two of them to have their private moment. While he waits, he turns to face me.

"You appear good. I appreciate your decision to wear jeans at the wedding. By the way, I'm being sincere about that as well. he claims. He may still feel uneasy around me since he is still learning how to be an uncle.

Mom and I came to the agreement that she would be fine with me not wearing a dress today if I had to wear one later. In addition, she dislikes tradition. I reply, grinning at him. He returns the smile and moves to embrace his older sister.

"You look wonderful, sis. You'll make a great Alpha Female, I have no doubt. Are you prepared, dad?

"Mom. It is now. when I give her a hug.

As the music starts, she inhales deeply and leans into her father's and brother's arms. In order for Cole to announce his wife as the Alpha Female of the pack, we are beginning as a human wedding. In case you didn't see, he is a little bit enthusiastic.

As she approaches the bend toward the chapel, the music starts as she inhales deeply. As Cole takes a big breath and begins to sob as she comes down the aisle, I follow her and carry the train of her veil. As his beautiful bride approaches him, he has a huge grin on his face and pride can be seen shining through his eyes. I am aware that my mother is grinning as she makes her way to the eternal life that the Luna above promised her. The chapel's huge windows and the sun streaming through them are evidence of how happy the Luna is with this coupling. The priest starts the ritual as soon as we get to the front.

"Today, Cole Peck and Ari Mora are getting married, so we've all come together to celebrate. Who is it that gives this man access to her? Priest speaks first.

"Her brother, her daughter, and I." Grandpa says while fighting back tears. Each boy gives her a cheek kiss before giving her to the man of her dreams.

"Though they are not what connects these two, the words that will be delivered here today are crucial. It's not even this ceremony. We're not here to initiate a relationship; rather, we're here to acknowledge one that already exists. We've gathered to see the growing love between Cole Peck and Ari Mora since they've already committed to being together.

"We are present to witness their declaration of love and dedication. This is a deed that is both as old as the human race and as fresh as the morning. Because it discusses the past, hopes for the future, personal existence, and collective existence. Marriage is a journey; it's a renunciation of one path in favor of another, risking what one is for what one might be in the process.

"Cole and Ari, do you come to this moment when you will be formally joined in marriage with delight and anticipation? Do you promise to treat one another with consideration, respect, and compassion, as well as to be open-minded and truthful with one another both now and in the future?

"We do." They both respond simultaneously.

"You've grown to truly and deeply love one another. You want to be married and start a family together because of the love you have for one another. You are committing yourself at this ceremony to one other's happiness and wellbeing. Marriage is a manifestation of trust. It must not be predicated on the naive expectation of what the other might or might not do or turn into. It must be founded on a strong conviction in both your own and the other person's inherent value. Your pledge today shows how devoted you are. Your marriage will only be recognized by the words said during this ceremony if your love and dedication for one another are strong enough to last. Today, in front of your families and friends, you declare your love for one another. We are happy for you and send our best wishes.

"Cole Peck and Ari Mora, as you have come here freely to give yourselves in marriage, do you now promise that you will love and honor each other as husband and wife?"

"We do."

Cole, say it again after me. I, [your name], take Ari Mora as my wife, to have and keep from this day forward, for better or for worse; for richer or poorer; in sickness and in health; to love and to cherish; till the end of our days.

Ari Mora, I, Cole Peck, take you to be my wife; to have and to hold from this day forward, for better or for worse; for richer or poorer; in sickness and in health; to love and to cherish; to the end of our days. With loving eyes and a trembling voice, he says.

Ari, say this after me. I, your name, take Cole Peck to be my husband; to have and to hold from this day forward, for better or for worse; for richer or poorer; in sickness or in health; to love and to cherish; till the end of our days.

Ari Mora declares, "I take you, Cole Peck, to be my husband; to have and to hold from this day forward, for better, for worse; for richer, for poorer; in sickness and in health; to love and to cherish; until the end of our days." She smiles up at him while having tears of delight rolling down her face.

Please give me the rings. He says, and I hand my parents both of them as I bring them forward.

"The ring represents an unbroken circle of love. Love has no start or finish when it is freely given. Since everyone is the giver and the receiver of love, there is no giver and no recipient. May the freedom and strength of your love be forever recalled by your rings! Cole, you're welcome to swap the rings.

As a symbol of my devotion to you until death do us part, I give you this ring. He says while grinning like he's devouring cheese and with tears running down his cheeks.

"Ari, you can swap the rings."

As a symbol of my devotion to you until death do us part, I give you this ring.

"I know you two are married. You are welcome to kiss the person. Before he can finish, the priest exclaims in disbelief as mom and dad embrace for a kiss in the center of the room. He smiles softly at them as they separate and face the spectators. "Mr. and Mrs. Cole Peck are now being introduced for the first time ever!"

As the crowd applauds, the priest moves to the side and the pack elder assumes his position. The parents bow to him as they turn around to face him.

We've just seen our Alpha marry his partner, as you can see. Are there any protesters among those who are knelt before our pack against Ari Peck being our Alpha Female? After a little period of silence, the elder resumes speaking to the group. Ri Peck. Rise. Do you voluntarily accept the duties that come with being an Alpha Female and the role that label entails? Do you pledge to uphold the pack's interests at all costs, to cherish the pack and its Alpha, and to persevere in the face of opposition to become the finest Alpha Female you are capable of being?

I vouch for it. Mom says, turning to face the elder and elevating her head so there is no hint of deceit in her eyes.

"Cassie, will you bring the blade forward?" When I do, I give the elder the blade. Ri Peck, put your hand up. I bind you to the Black Moon pack of Tennessee with this blade. Please stand. After poking my mother's finger and letting the knife soak up the blood, he says, linking her to the group. After being allowed to join the group in standing, Dad turns to face her and kisses the wound on her finger clean. In the traditional wedding fashion, they turn towards the group of people cheering them on and rush out of the chapel.

Alpha's Daughter Rejected: Chapter 25

Cassie's POV

The moment is drawing near. I'm putting on the dress I need to wear for my ceremonies while sitting in my chamber in the packhouse. We made the last-minute decision to have dad escort me down the aisle instead of a wedding. We don't need a lavish wedding ceremony right away; we just want to be together. The justice of the peace is taking care of everything since we did sign a marriage license. I made the decision to try since my dad is escorting me down the aisle. We won't have any issues as long as he respects my mother with respect.

We also chose to make vows and say them in private on our own. I doubt that I've ever been this enthusiastic about anything in my life. This was more exhilarating than even the prospect of finding my soul mate. I'm currently getting ready for my own Alpha Female ceremony while seated in a room with my mate's family and my just mated mother.

Cassandra pulls the garment bag out of the closet and says, "All right, time to get you into your dress."

~~~~~~~~~~~~

The outfit is of a traditional design that would be appropriate for a coronation. It was also the closest thing to a wedding gown my parents would see me in for a long. I force myself to hold my breath as Cass tightens the dress's corset and repress the impulse to touch my hair. This is quite strange for me because I'm not used to it being in my face and down.

"I want you to know that I sincerely appreciate everything you've done for me and everything you've done for my mother and me. There isn't a better family I could possibly join. I express my gratitude to the stunning gathering of women nearby. They all appear to be on the verge of crying. I'm overcome with fear when I observe their expressions.

Oh, Sweetheart, we are overjoyed that you are in our boy's life. You are stunning on the inside and out, and I'm glad you are with the family. She claims.

Emily puts a hand on her mother's shoulder and remarks, "Mom you switched languages."

"It's okay. I can speak Romanian. After meeting Whiskey and hearing him speak it, I picked it up. I admit with a small smile, "I was fascinated right away. I'm happy to be a part of the family, too.

"Alright. Remember to speak clearly and quietly, and refrain from touching your hair, as it is almost time. Your father should arrive shortly to give you away and take you down the aisle before the ceremony starts.

"Mom. I'm aware of how it operates. I assisted Alpha Lilly with hers while also planning yours and mine. Mom, I know how this is going to end, so breathe deeply and unwind. We can handle this. I say while the door is being knocked on.

"Are you ready to go, Cass?" Cole asks as he enters the space. He glances at me while having trouble breathing. "You appear stunning. That I wasn't there to witness you developing into the incredible young woman that you have become hurts my heart. I am overjoyed that you have allowed me to guide you into the future.

I approach him, give him a gentle smile, and take a deep breath. The women in the room rush to their seats and wait for us to walk down the aisle as we loop our arms together. The region behind the packhouse appears to be quite beautiful.

A cloth canopy was constructed, and lights were threaded across the fabric to illuminate it. The pack would run tonight at midnight across the woods in front of that location. Simple folding chairs were used as the chairs, and on the stumps were vases filled with yellow daisies. Together with other of the nearby Alphas who could break away from their packs for the occasion, guests filled the chairs from both our pack and Cole's pack. Everyone was grinning, and as my father and I headed down the aisle, some people started shooting pictures of us. My charming hubby was waiting at the very end of the seemingly endless aisle.

He had eyes filled with utter devotion as he gazed at me. His mismatched eyes made me fall in love with him more and more as they glistened. I almost fail to realize that we have moved to the front because I am so entranced by the way the light is shining on them. My father gives my husband and the ceremony my hands after kissing them.

The "Hidden Moon!" Whiskey declares, to loud applause from our pack. He grinned at the audience, and Axe and I grinned back at him. "We are here today to witness the union of our Alpha, Axe Dragoste, with Cassie Mora before God and the Luna above. Do you promise to love, cherish, and guard Axe and this pack with all of your heart until death takes you, Cassie, before God, the Luna above, and all of these witnesses?

I make this oath in the presence of God, the moon above, and each of these witnesses.

The blood knife, an axe. The ceremonial knife is passed from my love to his grandfather, and an incision is made in both of our hands. When we join them, a glow appears around us both, indicating that the Luna is happy. Whiskey grinned at us two. I give you, YOUR ALPHA PAIR, HIDDEN MOON OF NORTH CAROLINA.

As we engage in intense eye contact and are surrounded by yells, Axe asks me a crucial question.

"My love, may I kiss you?"

"You'd better, dearest husband," I thought.

Alpha's Daughter Rejected: Epilogue

Cassie's POV

"Have I told you how gorgeous you are, my love? inside and outside. Every day I'm more amazed by it. My charming husband says, carrying me in bridal fashion to our room. We're currently heading to say our vows after an after-party that lasted for approximately an hour. We agreed that it was for our ears only, as well as the ears of the goddess should she choose to listen, so we decided to perform it in secret.

"Even though you've brought it up, you've never given me an opportunity to tell you how incredible you are at anything you do. You are a young Alpha who managed to balance your responsibilities and your education with taking care of your family. You are without a doubt more magnificent than I am. He lays me on the bed as I say and kiss him. He lies down next to me, and for a few period, all we do is stare at one another.

"I love you more than life. You are entirely mine, and I was unable to find a better partner. You are my inspiration for living, my light amid the darkness. Nothing more than building a future with you is all I want in the world. envisioned by zeița as the protagonist. You are everything for mine. He says, pressing his forehead against mine and giving my nose a light kiss.

"That is the best thing that has ever happened to me," she said. Additionally, I was unable to find a better partner. Everything I need is known. I know my heart and chest are deghized. Zeița definitely made me happy when she put me on the tin. I add while smiling subtly. He gives me a passionate kiss while gazing lovingly into my eyes.

How about we begin with those seven children? I can't help but concur with what he says.

~~~~~~~~~~~~~~~~~

6 Months Later

Are we heading to your folks' house today? As he finishes getting ready, my spouse inquires.

Yes, my mother called to let me know she had some news to offer. I believe we have some as well. When we see them later today, we may let them know. Are you prepared to leave?

"Yes. You look gorgeous as ever, sweetie. May I?" I quickly kiss him after he says. He continues to ask before kissing me after six months of marriage.

After our quick kiss, I reply, "Ditto, my love." Every day, I find myself falling more and more in love with him, and just when I think I can't possibly love him any more, he does something idiotic, and all I can think is, "Yep. This is mine.

"Let's move forward now. A family supper ought to be held shortly. It would be lovely to see the family again.

But is there room at the table for the entire family? Eight people are represented by my parents, your parents, and four of my grandparents. Nine drinks with whiskey. Your sister, my uncle, your two brothers, and the two of us. plus the betas, gammas, and any other friends I failed to consider. Do we have a table that can accommodate more than twenty people?

"Let's have a picnic. The grandfather of your mother might not be able to endure spending too much time inside. He was a free spirit, after all. Whiskey won't survive very long inside, I'm aware of that. With that many people in one room, he would go crazy.

"Agreed. Okay, let's set up a picnic, but I want both packs to feel entirely at home there. They are also considered family.

"Good sounds. We'll schedule it for... the month's end? Do you believe that is effective for everyone?

There is only one way to learn. I don't want to be late, so hurry.

It didn't take long for mom and Cole to get to the agreed-upon meeting location, a cafe in a nearby city on shared territory. They were sitting on the terrace and taking advantage of the wind that the surprisingly warm day brought. Cole stood up when he first noticed us coming and greeted us. Mom adopted the same expression, seeming ecstatic and glowing.

"Cassie! Too much time has passed. My mother exclaims, putting her arms over my neck and almost suffocating me.

It has been about a week, Mom. Once a week, we have lunch together. I tell her while giving her a waist hug.

It's been a long week, I know. Okay, sit down. We have a lot to talk about.

It's fantastic to see you two again, Cassie and Axe.

As we sit, Axe responds, "You too Cole." I continue to call Cole other names while I nod to him. It's taking me some time to get used to the name because I've never had a father.

Mom nods to Cole and adds, "Ok, we have some really big and really surprising news." He responds with a tender grin. "We're expecting,"

They both appear to be about to cry, yet from their smiles I can tell they're joyful tears.

"I'm so happy for you, mom," I said.

"I'm grateful, my love. I didn't believe this could or would actually occur. We have another chance to be parents. Oh, I just want to cry. When she finished speaking, Cole gave her a consoling hug as tears began to fall down her face. Right now, they are content with one another. I'm very pleased for them both because they both deserve this.

Well, Ari, we also have some good news for you today. Says my hubby as he turns to face me. We exchange smiles before turning to face my parents.

We are also expecting.

Printed in Great Britain
by Amazon

38411276R00077